Gifted
In Kanyon Beach

the beach – from a child's only friend
to her source of unimaginable fulfillment

a novel by Dee Cohoon-Madore

DEELIGHTFUL READING

About the Author

A vivacious young senior, Dee lives in Digby, Nova Scotia. Being retired, she is free to escape into endless hours of writing.

Dee grew up in a relatively low-income family, in a rural community and was born fifth of ten children. Coming from a seriously dysfunctional family, her childhood was a very unhappy place to be. Her parents separated when she was eight years old, leaving her mother to raise a brood of kids on her

Dee Cohoon-Madore

own. Moving often, she had no place to call home. From her childhood memories, she can recall her mother wrapping dishes in old newspapers and packing them into a wooden barrel. There hadn't been much to move once you got past the dishes and linens. Household furnishings were sparsely made up of bits of living room furniture, beds, table and chairs and the barest of essentials. Life was far from easy for the family.

Marrying her childhood sweetheart, she moved to Toronto for several years. Although the marriage could have been a good one, it lasted for only seven years, but it brought her two beautiful children. Seemingly, she had already come full circle since now she had become the single mom. Living on a shoestring budget, she managed to see both her children graduate from high school and begin new lives and careers of their own.

The empty nest syndrome had encouraged her to focused on pursuing further education. With an entrepreneurial spirit, she formed a company and operated a successful business. It was during her business years that she met her future husband.

After remarrying, she began to focus seriously on her writing. She had notebooks and scraps of writing, but nothing really materialized until she began to write her first novel, 'Gifted.' Her next book, titled 'Tidbits, Tips & Treasures,' is a self-help book meant to have something for everyone. She has since completed

'Gypsy Heart' and made it available on her newly redesigned website. She has already turned her attention to her next storytelling adventures, 'The Grand Manor' and 'Timeless Love.' Two new books will soon be available, and Dee hopes that you will let her know your thoughts after settling in with any of her novels, by leaving a comment at her website. She reads and personally replies to every bit of correspondence so, don't be shy.

Dee thanks everyone for their love and support, and hopes you enjoy reading her works as much as she enjoyed writing them.

Dreams

We all have hopes and dreams for ourselves. I am one of those dreamers. One of my dreams was to write a book, and that dream has come true. There had always been a nagging in the back of my mind that I was forgetting to do something. Even though, over the years, I had written poetry, songs, short stories, and children's books, all of which are still in my computers and notebooks. That nagging did not go away until I began my first novel, Gifted. I was extremely proud when I had it finished. This story began from a dream which I wrote down on four sheets of paper, the next morning, while the dream was still fresh in my mind. From those four pages, my book unfolded, and my dream was realized between the covers of the novel. Page after page was written with what I called my storybook pencil. It was only when I had it in my hand that the words flowed to paper. The unedited version was done in less than three weeks. It was a joy to write, and since it started out as a short dream, my next dream is that someday I might see my story made into a family movie. It would be an absolute dream to see my characters come to life on screen.

I once dabbled in my own fashion line, which is still on paper in my filing cabinet. I loved to get my drawing pad out and sit in my lounge chair and sketch clothing of all kinds. From evening wear to pajamas and everything in between. As a matter of fact, I am not a great sketcher by any stretch of the imagination, but as long as I am holding a pencil, I am in a good place.

We all have our dreams and so should the readers of Gifted. I hope you enjoy my book and I look forward to and encourage you to post a comment on my website. I had great pleasure in creating it; everyone reading it, thus far, loved it. It is my hope that you get as much enjoyment from reading it as I did in writing it. I am currently working on my second novel, Gypsy Heart. It will be added to the website when completed, and a snippet of Gypsy Heart will be posted to give you a taste of what is coming.

Dedication

Gifted, is dedicated to my God and my own special Guardian Angel who have been ever present with me. Without their guidance and everlasting love, my life could have taken unimaginable turns and not led me to this place of Peace, Tranquility, and Creativity, I now enjoy.

Acknowledgements

Once again, I give thanks to my God for giving me the gift of words and enabled me to turn them into stories for my readers to enjoy, and hopefully relate to.

I wish to extend a sincere and heartfelt thank you to Cedar Springs, my publisher, web designer and cover creator. Thank you for always being there for me and for tirelessly giving your time and advice, and for being my 'go to guy.' Without you this book would not have made it to print.

And, to my dedicated readers; thank you for your patience, your gracious comments on my web site and most especially, for requesting to be on the list for future book releases. Next on the list is JOY which is a little different from my usual and I hope it brings you as much entertainment reading as it has given me in creating it.

Gifted

in Kanyon Beach

He was leaning on a post when he happened to look up and see the face of a sad young girl looking down onto the beach from a second story window. Sensing unhappiness, he knew she was not looking for anything except maybe a friend. Knowing what was there, he wanted her to see it too. He felt she needed to find joy and a purpose which is why he's chosen her. Watching from below, he knew she'd be unable to see him until such time that he became visible to her.

Sending a glistening speck of recognition up to her, he hoped she'd see it. Instantly, her eyes caught a glimpse of something, and it was exactly what he'd hoped she'd see. Smiling to himself, he was quite satisfied that she'd made the connection. Seeing her scurry away from the window, he knew she'd be coming outside, and he waited for her to come around the corner to the spot where he'd shown her.

She was an adorable little thing with golden hair. He noticed that she was dressed in a suitable fashion, but nothing that looked like it was worth much. The dress she wore was ankle length, and over top of it, she wore a pinafore with large patch pockets. He guessed it must be something she'd worn to keep her dress clean. She wore black ankle high shoe booties, and a bonnet hung down her back and held on by ribbons that were tied around her throat. *'It should have been on her head to protect her delicate skin from the sun,* he thought. She reminded him of a little rag-a-muffin, and maybe that is why he had chosen her...

Watching her, she bent down to pick up what she'd spotted from the window. Pulling a white, neatly folded hankie from her pocket, she began to clean the dirt off her treasure. She polished the piece until it was sparkling and bright in color. When she finished cleaning it and was satisfied with it, she dropped it into her pocket. He allowed her to catch sight of another shiny object and he watched as her face brightened when she picked it up. He smiled at the pleasure he was bring. Still holding her hankie, she rubbed and polished her new piece until she was satisfied with it. Dropping it into her pocket, she stuffed the hankie in on top of her treasures. Just as she'd turned to leave, he made himself known to her and hoped he would not frighten her as he stood leaning against the lamp post...

~

As a child, Eden Thomas lived in a house that was situated on a beautiful waterfront property on Kanyon Beach. Her bedroom was on the second floor, and on the same side as the beach so she could watch the tides come and go. One day, while she was playing in her room, she'd gone over to the window and noticed that the tide was out. The beach was her favorite place to be, and although she was never a collector of rocks and seashells and other beach-like things, she just loved being there. It gave her a feeling like no other, and she claimed it to be her own.

Standing in her window, she looked down at the beach. Suddenly, her eyes caught sight of something shining between the rocks, and she wondered what it could be. Racing down the stairs, out the door, and down the front steps to the sidewalk, she rounded the corner to the beach. Standing at the spot where she thought she saw it, she looked up at her window trying to orient herself as to where she'd seen whatever it was that had caught her eye. Looking from the rocks to the window several times, she saw it. *'There it is!'* she thought. It was lodged between two rocks, and the excitement began as she stooped to pick it up. Turning it over several times, she looked at all sides and saw that it was a shiny but dirty piece of red glass.

Thinking it might look a little better, she pulled a perfectly folded hankie from her pocket, gave it a quick shake to unfold it and began rubbing off the sand and dirt. She was glad now that her mother insisted she carry a hankie. She had always told her she would never know when she would need one and today she did. Blowing as much sand off as she could, she began to rub and polish the piece of red glass until it was as shiny as a new penny. Dropping it into her big square pocket, she caught sight of another piece only this one looked as if it was purple. Moving a few small stones around, she managed to get the piece out. Working just as hard to clean and polish it, she knew it was just as pretty as the first one. Dropping it into her pocket with the red one, she stuffed her hankie in on the top of them for safe keeping. Feeling satisfied with what she had found, she'd come to realize this could become her new hobby. It was going to be fun to beach comb and try to find more pieces of what she referred to as beach glass. This was something she was truly going to love, and it involved the place she most loved to be... her beach.

She would not have time to search for more glass today. She saw that the tide was coming it was her cue to leave. From the time she was old enough to go outside alone, her mother had warned her that when she saw the water coming in, she had to leave immediately. Reminding her that it rushed in quickly and didn't leave much time to escape. She knew if she did not want to be banned from the beach forever she'd had to obey the rules. Turning to leave she saw a man standing nearby...

3

He was someone she hadn't seen around the neighborhood, and it startled her. Stopping in her tracks, she felt a little more than scared and bordered on fright. Before panicking, she took a deep breath and looked him up and down. He was dressed kind of weird, but he was clean although bedraggled looking. He wore rough looking and tattered shoes, pants that were wide and ragged on the bottom edges, gloves that had the fingers either cut off or worn out, she could not be sure which. He wore a grey three-quarter length coat and a funny looking hat on his head with longish blond hair sticking out. As she took a closer look at him, she noticed he had a whitish, blond, short stubbly beard that looked like he hadn't shaved in several days.

He was leaning against a lamp post smiling at her, and she tensed up as fear bit at the back of her throat. She was close enough to him that he saw her large, adoring green eyes with scatterings of dark blue and her skin was flawless.

Not knowing what else to do, she froze on the spot and waited. He was standing close to where she'd needed to pass. Sensing her fear, he wanted to put her mind at ease as quickly as possible before she panicked and ran off.

"Hello Little One," he said, softly, "don't be afraid." He had a twinkle in his eyes and a soothing voice that almost reassured her that he was harmless, but she stayed on guard anyway. Not moving from his spot, he made no sudden moves and didn't try to get closer to her. Wanting to gain her trust him, he stayed in the same position as when she'd first noticed him. "My name is San, what's yours Little One?"

"Eden," she said, and then asked, "what kind of a name is Sand?"

4

He laughed and said, "My name is San, and my last name is Taman, but you can call me San-Ta."

Eden's face lit up with surprise and was delighted that she'd met Santa! The joyous look on her face told him immediately that she had misunderstood him. Before he'd had a chance to say anything, she gave a shout.

"Santa? You're Santa?" she asked as her face broke into a smile.

Assuring her that he was not 'the' Santa and told her she could call him San-Ta or just San, as most of his 'secret friends' did. She hadn't caught the 'secret friends' part of it right away.

"Can I see what you have in your pocket, Eden?"

Eden wasn't sure what to do. *'How did he know she had treasures in her pocket?'* she wondered. She gave him a frown like no other he had ever seen, and it made him smile.

"It's ok Little One," he said, "I would just like to look at them, and I promise I won't touch them if you don't want me too."

Feeling quite certain she could trust him, Eden took out her hankie and then reached deep into the very bottom of her pocket. Scooping up the two pieces of glass in her tiny hand, she made a fist for safety and brought them out. Stretching out her arm, she looked up at him and slowly turned her hand over and opened up her tiny fist. There in the palm of her wee small hand were two magnificent pieces of precious stones. One, a dark red ruby and the other a deep purple amethyst.

He hadn't asked her where she got them since he already knew, and he didn't touch them, because he knew exactly what she had.

"These are very beautiful, Eden," he said looking up down at her.

She closed her fingers around her treasures and said, "Thank you, San-Ta."

"Would you consider selling me your treasures?"

Looking up at him and then down at the pieces, she frowned and became very protective of her treasures. "But, I just found them!" she said, possessively.

"Yes, I know you did, Little One," he said speaking softly as he noticed she was getting agitated. Trying to put her at ease, he continued. "I would like to buy them from you, and if you find more pieces, I will buy them also."

Eden didn't usually ask too many questions, but she had one, and she wanted it answered. She was not giving up her treasures to a stranger that easily. "Why do you want my beach treasures, San-Taman?"

Looking down at her, he smiled as she stared up at him, determined for an answer. Slipping the treasures back into her pocket, she crossed her arms and waited for him to speak. He loved her spunk. Seeing the look of determination on her face, he knew she was not going to budge until she got the answer she was looking for and one that she'd be satisfied with.

"Well, Little One," he began with the same gentleness as always. "You know, money is something that many people do not have a lot of, and I think the same is true at your house. So, if you'll consider selling me your treasures, I promise you, that in the near future, you will want for nothing. How does that sound to you?"

Her family wasn't exactly poor, but she knew that what her father brought home was barely enough to meet their needs.

She didn't quite understand everything he'd just said, but she pretended that she had. Nodding her head, she reluctantly agreed to sell her newly found treasures.

"I will buy your treasures on a couple of conditions Eden." Squinting at him, she wasn't certain what 'conditions' meant so, she waited for him to finish speaking.

Smiling at her enquiring glance, he asked her if she knew what 'conditions' were.

"No, not really," she said honestly.

"It's kind of like rules that are set in place, for us to follow. Does that explain it better for you?"

Nodding her head, he began again. "The first condition is, if you find more treasures, like the ones in your pocket," he said pointing in that direction, "and no matter what color they are, you will sell them to me. Do you understand what I just said?"

Nodding again, she waited for him to continue.

"The second condition is, you must not tell anyone about me unless you know for certain they have your gift..."

"My gift?" she asked, not quite understanding him.

"Yes Eden, your gift. You may not have realized it, but you are the only one who can find these treasures and that, Little One, a rare gift."

"Really?" she said, squealing with delight while taking in what he'd just told her.

"Yes, really," he said smiling at her. "And Little One, not only do you have a special gift to find these treasures, you are also the only one who can see me."

"I am?" she said with a sobering look on her face.

"Yes, indeed you are. So, what do you think of my conditions Little One?" he asked, "Do you think you can keep our secret?"

She thought about it for only a few seconds before answering him. "I'm sure I can, San Taman."

Reaching out his hand as a gesture to solidify their deal, she looked at it for a few seconds. Nodding his head once, as she looked up at him for reassurance, she reached out and laid her hand in his. When he felt her tiny hand touch his, he knew in his heart what a special child she was as they shook hands to seal their new partnership. Reaching deep into his grey three-quarter length coat pocket, he presented her with several coins. Stretching out her hand, he dropped them into her waiting palm. When she saw the coins, her chin dropped, and her eyes widened as she looked at them in her tiny hand.

"Wow!!! San Taman, that's a lot of money!"

"Yes, it is," he said as he waited. In turn, Eden dug into her pocket for the two pieces of treasures. Smiling up at him, she dropped them into his waiting palm to complete their deal.

"When you find more pieces, I'll be back with more money for you, ok?"

"Yes!" she said as she wrapped her coins up tightly in her dirty hankie so that they wouldn't jingle.

And this was day that had Eden begun her secret journey with San Taman.

Knowing it was time to go home, she hurried up the steps to her front door. Turning once, she saw San holding his finger up to his pursed lips. Smiling at him, she nodded. Turning the doorknob to let herself in, she turned to say goodbye to San, but there was no one there! Looking up and down the street, Eden was in disbelief as she brought her eyes back to the lamp post. Staring at the vacant street for a few puzzling moments, she tried to figure out where he had gone and how he'd disappeared so fast. Frowning for a few seconds, she opened the door and went inside. Stopping only long enough to say hi to her mother, she went directly upstairs to her room. Laying the beach-stained dirty hankie out on her bed, she carefully unfolded it as sand and dirt spilled out onto her bed. Amazed at all the coins that lay in her hankie, she began to count...

Eden was not used to having money of her own, until today. It excited her as she went in search for a special box to keep her secret coins in. She wasn't quite sure if she was excited about her coins or the fact that it was a secret. After a little bit of pondering, she realized it was a little bit of both.

~

She found an old wooden box that was shaped like a chest that had once belonged to her mother. She had given it to Eden when she was old enough to play with it. At the time when it was new, it was filled with her mother's odd pieces of cheap jewelry. When her mom had graduated to a real jewelry box, she'd given the old chest to Eden. She didn't have a lot of playthings which made the chest very special even though she'd never put anything in it. She still kept the chest as a reminder that gifts were rare from her mother and this was her chance to use it. Eden had felt that by keeping the chest, it made her feel as close to her mother as she was ever going to get.

Counting her coins again, she gathered them up, put them in the chest and closed the lid. For a hiding place, she slipped it under several layers of homemade quilts at the very bottom of her trunk that sat at the foot of her bed. Just then, she had a moment of panic! *'How will I find San Taman the next time... if there is a next time...?'* she wondered.

~

Eden was at her window again a few days later, and the tide was out. Being high up, she had a great view of the beach. The Brownstone that she lived in made it seem like she was on the third floor instead of the second. All the rooms had at least ten-foot ceilings and thick floors to prevent sounds from traveling from one storey to the other. It was a grand old place, and she loved it here. She did not know what she would ever do if she were not living near her beach.

Standing there with darting eyes, she frantically searched the beach. She was not sure if she would ever again find more pieces of 'glass' and she was disappointed when she thought she might not. She stood there with hopes that something, anything would catch her eye and finally... *'Oh yes...! There it was!' There was something shining down there!'* Convinced and filled with the same excitement as the first time, she raced down the stairs and out to the beach. *'Was there something there or was she just imagining it?'* she wondered. She went in search for the spot where she thought she'd seen the piece and sure enough, there it was! Picking it up from between the rocks, she saw that this one was a different color. Finding a small pool of water that was left from the tide, she swished the glass around in it and removed some of the caked-on dirt. Pulling out her hankie, she began cleaning and polishing it until it shined. It was the deepest green she had ever seen. Her only thought was how very beautiful it was. Standing on the same spot, she turned only slightly and saw another piece glistening in the sun. Putting the green piece in her pocket for safe keeping, she bent down to pick up the other piece. Giving it a quick swish in the same puddle, she began to rub and clean the new piece. It became very shiny and clean but, to her disappointment, it had no color to it at all, and she thought it was just an ordinary piece of broken glass that had washed in with the tide. She put it in her pocket with the other one anyway. Still thinking it was just a piece of broken glass, her heart sank. Suddenly, San's voice popped into her head, and she remembered him telling her not to worry about the color, he wanted it anyway. Preparing herself to go back inside she saw yet another piece, and her heart soared! With her hankie still in her hand, she picked up the piece and began to

11

clean it up too and found that it was a beautiful deep blue. She rubbed and polished it until it sparkled. Feeling very pleased with her findings, she turned away to go home, and she almost ran into him.

"San-Ta, look at what I've found!" she squealed as she reached into her pocket with delight. Reaching into her pocket, she pulled them out. Grinning broadly, she stretched her arm out as far as it would go and carefully opened her hand. San Taman was pleased with what he saw as he stared at a beautiful deep green emerald, a good size diamond, and a luscious blue sapphire.

"My goodness, Eden, how very pretty they are and what a fine job you've done of cleaning them up!" Feeling very proud of herself, she was glad that she had taken the extra time cleaning each piece.

"Are we still in agreement, Eden?"

"Oh, yes we are, San Taman."

Reaching into his pocket again, he drew out a little sack that was pulled together at the top with a string. Holding it out, Eden took it, and in return, she handed over the three treasures.

She couldn't wait to put the coins with the others in her money chest. Looking down at the bag that held her coins, she raised her head to say goodbye to San, but he was nowhere around. Shading her eyes against the sun, she looked up one side of the beach and down the other, but he was not there. Sputtering to herself, she realized she was going to have to figure out where he went because this was beginning to get very old.

Hurrying up the stairs to her room, she opened her trunk. Moving the bedding aside, she reached in and felt around until she found her money chest. Opening up the chest, she dumped all the coins out on her bed to look at them again and knowing there was one hundred dollars in her secret stash. Pulling open the strings on her new little sack of coins, she dumped them out on her bed too. She'd never felt the need to count her money on the street because she'd developed a trust in San Taman that even she didn't understand. She'd deemed him trustworthy and had taken it for granted that he was as honest with her as she was with him. Tallying up the pieces she'd gotten today, she was astounded when she counted two hundred and fifty dollars! Eden was beside herself. She realized San Taman had given her fifty dollars for each piece of 'glass' that she'd found! That was a lot of money to her, and she secretly stashed them in the chest with the other coins and placed it safely back inside her trunk...

Eden searched for treasures at every opportunity. She couldn't wait to get home from school to go out and comb the beach. She was often disappointed on the days when she'd get home, and the tide was already in. At high tide, Eden knew it would take at least six to eight hours to low tide. On those days it made it impossible for her to beach comb. Rules were in place at home for Eden and homework had to be finished before she was allowed to go out on the beach. Sitting in her room doing homework, she would often glance out her window at the water-filled beach. Her thoughts were about when she'd be able to treasure hunt again and when she would have another chance to see San. He had become an important part of her life, and she treasured her time with him. He was about the only contact she'd had with an adult, and he had always treated her as his equal even though she was much younger. She not only loved to hunt for treasures but just knowing it would give her a few minutes with San gave her something to look forward to. She felt something for San, and she never wanted to lose it. She was always amazed at how fast he'd disappear whenever their transactions were completed. Thinking it over for several minutes, she'd developed a plan for the next time he appeared. She'd decided that when it came time to do their transaction, she would hang on to her treasures just a little bit longer than usual and that way she could spend a few more minutes with him.

She could hardly wait for the weekends to roll around. No homework and two days to go out on the beach and collect her treasures. Maybe not every day or even every weekend but several times a week there would be many opportunities to collect, clean and polish treasures for San. And, as he'd promised, he was always there whenever she'd be lucky enough to find some. Not only was she looking forward to some beach time, but she was also looking forward to seeing him again.

2

Eden Thomas was such a joy to be around. It made San happy when she collected a few treasures. It gave him a reason to spend time with her again. They were great friends by now and even from the very beginning, he knew he'd made an excellent choice.

She was growing up and the last couple of years made a difference in her appearance. She was not quite the little girl that he'd met on the beach, but her personality remained unchanged. Their partnership had already grown into several years and blossomed into a true friendship.

She still lit up when she saw him, and it made his day when he had a chance to be with her for even a few minutes.

Figuring out her plan for him a long time ago, and had noticed that after a few transactions, she'd deliberately put off passing over the treasures right away. Bringing it to her attention, she laughed and told him that he always disappeared right after they exchanged goods for money. So, to spend more time with him, she had decided to hang on to the treasures a few minutes longer. San knew their friendship was going to last a long, long time and in the not too distant future she was going to need him, and he would be there for her.

Time meant nothing to San, but he continued to watch the changes in Eden as each year passed. She was turning into a beautiful young woman right before his eyes. The one thing that hadn't changed was her bubbly personality.

As a typical teenager, she was learning to lightly apply make-up to enhance her finer points. Using a jade color pencil, she'd underline her lower lids to bring out the green tones in her eyes, touched a brush to her cheekbones and dab her lips with a dash of pink. In a more fashionable sense, she also became wiser and dressed more stylishly.

On her leisurely days, weather permitting, he'd see her in a pair of faded blue jeans, rolled up at the bottoms, bare foot in her runners, along with a warm sweater, and off she'd go to her favorite place. Now and then San walked with her to keep her company, but mostly he just let her be and waited for his time. Occasionally, bringing a book, she'd find a sheltered spot, settle in and read for hours. She'd had an innate sense of time when she was at the beach. For many years, she'd kept such a close eye on the tide that it was instinctive now. Being warned so many times, as a child, it was indelibly imprinted in her brain. She'd always allowed herself plenty of time to get back home safely. San was usually hanging around somewhere keeping an eye on her. Most of the time she couldn't see him, but she felt his presence almost always, and she'd never felt alone since meeting San.

She was in her last year of school, and she could not believe how fast the time had passed. She often daydreamed of what she would do when she was finished. Would she leave home? Would she stay? Would she even go if she had the chance? So much to dream about and she wondered when the time came to leave... would she? San knew what she was thinking, and he knew that she was dreaming the wrong dreams.

~

Well into her teens, Eden could still be found walking the beach in search of treasures. It was not just 'pretty glass' to her anymore, and she was aware of what she was gathering. Still, in partnership, she had never asked San what he did with the gems, nor did she care. He was true to his word and was there when he was needed, and she was happy with that. Each time she collected pieces, San appeared out of nowhere, and they'd exchange goods for coins. It was magical how he'd take the beach glass, and suddenly, they appeared as gems.

She took San's appearances for granted now, being the loyal and trusted friend that he was, she knew he would always be around. She didn't know where he came from and could not figure out where he went, so she stopped trying.

As she grew older, San still looked the same as the day they met except for his attire. He didn't look quite so bedraggled and appeared quite stylish. Perhaps he had been in style back then, and she had been too young to know what was, or was not, fashionable.

Long ago, she had opened the trunk at the foot of her bed and removed all the quilts, except one. Having collected hundreds of thousands of coins over the years, she'd stopped counting. Laughing at herself, she felt like a pirate with a trunk full of gold. She didn't know what she was ever going to do with it, but there it was, and it belonged to her. She'd kept that one quilt to lay over the top of her stash.

During their partnership, San had raised the price of each piece several times, and she still didn't check to see how much the sack contained until she got back to her room. She never questioned why there was more than when they first made their deal, she just accepted whatever he gave her. No one ever questioned what was in her trunk, and no one ever asked to look inside. It was as if it did not exist to anyone except to her. She had outgrown her tiny money chest long ago, and now she just lifted the trunk lid, moved the quilt aside and tossed the coins in and she had never given up their secret.

And so, the trunk contents continued to grow...

After graduating high school, Eden knew she'd never have to go out and look for work. With all the money in her trunk, what would be the point? She certainly didn't need money so why take a job away from someone who did. Deciding to take courses, she learned how to sew. Her plan was to become a seamstress so she could have a stay-at-home job through which she would earn a modest income. This seemed like the perfect solution to keep her close to her beach and her treasures. It would also enable her to beach comb when she chose, still be at home, and earn a few dollars at the same time. It had to appear as though she was working in case she needed to spend coins for something unexpected. She had never spent a single coin that she'd gotten from San.

~

Once her course was completed, she posted an ad on the local bulletin boards to let people know there was a seamstress, with reasonable rates, in the neighborhood. Word spreading of her talents, she soon met people from all walks of life. Coming to her door, they had ragged pieces of clothing in need of alterations or repairs. For many who showed up, they looked as if they were in bad financial shape and some of the pieces of clothing were in even worse shape. Having a big heart and deep pockets, and many times Eden had altered her customers' garments at no charge. Her sewing talent was meant for her to earn an income, but she was well aware that she didn't need their money to sew up a seam, hem a skirt or put a patch on a ragged elbow or the knee of a pair of trousers. Most times the folks who brought mending could not afford to buy new things or replace their ragged clothes from a thrift shop, so she did not have the heart to take their money. In fact, to lessen their burden, she'd take a few coins, from her trunk, and place them in different pockets of the men's trousers so they wouldn't jingle. She imagined the surprised looks on their faces when they put them on again. Many of the women's dresses had pockets as well, and she'd do the same for them by dropping a few coins into each pocket after mending them. She'd then package them up neatly in brown paper and tie them with string. When they offered her money for her work, she'd make excuses that she did not have change and that she would see them the next time. She'd often see sheer relief on their faces knowing they still had a dollar or two for a few more days. Her customers loved her, and Eden knew if they needed their ragged clothes mended then they could not afford to pay her. It wasn't a difficult concept to figure out if they could afford it, they'd likely buy new things and use these rags as just that... rags.

This was the beginning of using her coins toward good works.

Feeling blessed, Eden felt good about being able to give a few coins here and there. She knew for certain they were needed so badly by these poor people. The memory of San's word still echoed in her head as she heard him say, "You will want for nothing," and after all these years, she has wanted for nothing.

Whenever she had time to beach comb, he was always there when she got back. She continued to look forward to their brief meetings. Sometimes he would meet her on the beach when she finished her hunt, and they would do their exchange while they chatted briefly. These were the two favorite things for Eden, her beachcombing for treasures and meeting up with San. While she waited for him and out of the blue, words drifted to her mind.

My life consists of two kinds of Time
The Time when I am with you
And the Time when I am waiting to be with you again

Thinking about it, she thought the words were appropriate and wondered why they'd even enter her head as she waited for San to arrive. This is what her life did consist of, and it had for as long as she could remember. He still had not changed much since they first met although it seemed like he was still keeping up with the fashion trends. Maybe the 'bedraggled' look he'd back then was in fashion for that era because he didn't look so bad now. Of course, she had been only a little girl then, too, and anyone over twenty would have been considered ancient to her. He still seemed to be a bit older than she was, but it didn't stop her heart from fluttering whenever she saw him. If she were honest with herself, she would admit that he was very attractive and if she were not careful with her thoughts, she would have herself convinced that she might even have a crush on him. She was just as anxious to see him now as she was back then. She had learned to trust him from the first day, and he had never let her down. Maybe she was just attracted to the honest and trusting part of him and the fact that he had always accepted her for who she was. He had always been the one constant in her life.

~

Eden spent the better part of the day at her sewing machine and needed a break. She went across the hall to her bedroom window to check the tide situation. Seeing that it had turned and was on its way back in, she still had lots of time to take a walk. The same excitement began to build inside her as she pulled on a warm sweater, stuck a hankie in her pocket and headed outside. Taking a better look at the tide, she calculated her time while glanced around at the scenery that nature had unfolded before her. She came to the realization, a long time ago, that she felt as much a part of this beach as she did with her own family, probably more so if truth be known. Walking for at least half an hour, she wasn't quite ready to go home. Climbing up on a huge rock, in the lee of the wind, she just sat there taking in the beauty around her.

She was in deep thought about her long relationship with her beach, how much she loved it here and about her life in general when suddenly and quietly San's voice broke the silence.

"Hello Little One," he said in that quiet, peaceful voice of his.

"Hi, San! It's nice to see you. How about pulling up a rock and sitting with me for a little while?"

"I would love to Eden," he said as he sat down on a rock beside her. They were at a place in their friendship where neither one had to strain for conversation. If they didn't have anything to say, then they sat in silence and still enjoyed each other's company. Eden felt peaceful when San was around her. From the first time she looked into his eyes, that peaceful, easy feeling was there. She had known San for almost fifteen years, and he had not changed in personality from day one. Thinking about it now, she realized she spent more time with him than she did with her father, and her thoughts wandered back to her parents.

She found it rather sad that she'd never spent much time with them. They were, in reality, almost strangers to her. They rarely had a conversation, seldom ate a meal as a family or went out together. There was never a time that she could remember them asking her how her day went. She didn't know anything about their likes or dislikes or even if they had friends.

Recently, they were gone a lot of the time now, but she never knew where they went or when they'd be home, and they never bothered to tell her. She often wondered if she even existed to them. *'Had they forgotten that they even have a daughter? Perhaps she did not belong to them, who knew! Was it that she was so unlovable or were they?'* she thought. She had no other siblings, so she did not have to fight for their attention; there was no one to fight against. *'Why do couples have children if they don't have time for them?'* she wondered.

She'd grown up being fed, clothed, a roof over her head and in a nice enough house in a relatively safe neighborhood, but that was it. She felt like an obligation and nothing more. *'It was a horrible lonely feeling that children should not have to experience,'* she remembered. *'If she was ever lucky enough to have a family of her own someday,'* she thought, *'she was certain she'd never want them to feel the way she'd felt growing up, and still did. Their lives would mean something to her, and she'd do whatever she possibly could to let them know how much she loved them.'*

San felt her thoughts drifting to an unpleasant place, but he sat in silence while they ran through her mind. She didn't like to dwell in these places often, or she would probably find it too depressing. She'd refused to allow her parents to have that much power over her but sometimes it pulled her back in. San knew it was time to speak... "Eden?" he said breaking the silence, "we should head back now, the tide is coming." She had been so absorbed in her thoughts, she totally forgot about the time and the tide! If San had not been with her, she would have been caught in the tide!

"Thank you, San, I'm so glad you were here."

"So am I Little One," he said as they climbed down off their rocks and headed back up toward the safety of the beach. There was not much conversation on the way back, but Eden was thinking about the trouble she would have been in if San had not been with her this afternoon.

She had never done that before, she had always paid close attention to the tides. The only thing she could relate it to was that having the comfort of San with her. Knowing he'd take care of her, she'd just allowed herself to relax for a change, and she'd gotten lost in her thoughts. Whatever the reason was, it had sure frightened her, and it was something she would not likely forget anytime soon. The thought of being caught by the tide had always frightened her and with good reason. If it were to come

23

to that, there was no place for her to go to wait it out unless she knew how to climb a mountain high stone wall that had been erected years ago to prevent erosion. Her house was just above her, but she'd never get to it.

"Thank you again San, I guess I got lost in my thoughts and I'm so thankful you happened to be here with me."

"Not to worry Little One, I'm always here with you."

She looked up at him, smiled and wished she could put her arms around him at this moment. Actually, she couldn't recall ever touching him except for when she was a little girl, and she remembered their handshake to seal their partnership.

3

Eden was in her mid-twenties, and once again her parents were away on another one of their mysterious trips and had been away from home for several weeks. She never knew when to expect them back, but she was beginning to feel uneasy.

Knowing she was going to need him, San was close by but out of sight.

Eden was upstairs in her sewing room working on alterations when the doorbell rang. Thinking it was one of her customers, she raced to the front door. Opening it, her heart sank as she stood facing two police officers.

"Eden Thomas?" one of the officers asked.

"Yes, what's this about?"

"May we come inside?"

Stepping aside, they entered the foyer then she closed the door and showed them into the den. Nearly lost her balance, her heart pounded wildly, as she waited for one of them to speak.

"Please sit down, Ms. Thomas," one of the officers insisted. As if she were a robot, she sat.

"We're sorry to have to inform you of this matter, but your parents were involved in a fatal plane crash yesterday. Since they were out of the country, we are just now receiving the information."

Feeling the strength go out of her body, Eden was glad she was sitting down. "When will my parents' remains be back in the country?" Eden asked as soon as she was able to speak.

"I'm afraid they won't be, you see, they were in a small twin-engine plane that crashed and burned, and there is nothing left of the wreckage."

"Then how can you be certain my parents were on the plane?" she asked.

The officer in charge told her the information was filed at the airport. They had hired the plane and in doing so, the identification of all passengers on board, including their passport numbers, was needed, and their names were on the list. Eden was horrified at what she was hearing, but there it was. Her parents were gone, both of them... just like that... gone...

"We're very sorry for your loss."

"Thank you for coming officers."

"Again, we are very sorry for your loss Ms. Thomas, but before we leave, is there someone we can call to come and be with you?"

Off to one side of the room, she thankfully caught sight of San. Being the only one in the room who could see him, she looked straight at him knowing he was the strength she needed at this moment. San saw and felt the tremendous amount of pain she was having.

"No, there is no one to call," she said, fixing her eyes on San. "Thank you again," she said as she walked them to the door. Tipping the bill of their hat, they gave their condolences again on the way out. Trying to absorb the conversation, she slowly closed the door and laid her back against it for a few seconds. A feeling of familiarity caused her to straighten up. Raising her eyes, she saw San standing in front of her. She never thought twice as she walked into his arms and sobbed into his chest. Standing in complete silence, he held her and tried his best to protect her from the pain while she cried. Her heart was breaking, for the parents, she never really knew.

Eden became filled with mixed emotions realizing she was in San's arms. She was sad about the loss of her parents yet this feeling she was having, being held by San, was filling her with a different kind of emotion. She wondered how a person could possibly feel sad and happy at the same time. This was the first time, since she was a child, that she could remember touching him since the day they'd initiated their partnership. Yet, somehow it felt normal for him to be there, and now actually, he was all she had. She'd never see her parents again, and even though she rarely saw them when they were alive, this was coldly final.

Eden could not come up with a valid reason to have a memorial service for her parents. '*Who would she invite and who would actually attend?*' she wondered. Neither of her parents had ever mentioned relatives to her, and she had no idea if they had friends and it made her feel very much alone in the world. The only thing to do for them now was to write up obituaries, in case there were others who cared about their passing, and give it to the local newspaper... how very, very sad...

27

~

The reading of their Will was brief and to the point. They'd left her everything they had which was very little and consisted of no money, just the house and it's furnishing at 56 Garden Place, in Kanyon beach. The wheels began to turn in Eden's head as thoughts began to form. *'If there were no other family members, that she was aware of, then it meant no one knew of her parents' financial status. So that would also mean no one knew if she was left a pauper or an heiress!'* Except for the few coins she'd dropped into her customers' pockets she had not used the money for anything else...

Was it time to open the trunk...?

In the very early spring, following the accident, Eden's heart was beginning to heal from the loss of her parents and to keep herself busy and occupied she began to work in her mother's small garden that now belonged to her. This was not going to be an easy task since, every aspect of the garden, she saw her mother's hard work from years past. At every turn, thoughts of her mom were with her while she prepared the garden and set out to make it hers. Still, she could not believe that she never knew what it was like to play here as a child. It gave her feelings of sadness, knowing that her mother was gone forever, and she had absolutely no memories of being here with her to share this lovely space.

Her house sat on a patch of ground with an embankment at the end of it with a safety fence around the property. It had a beautiful ocean view and large enough for a fair-sized backyard patio and gardens. Before this, though, the only water views she saw were from her bedroom window. All that had changed since these grounds belonged to her. She spent hours raking up old leaves and digging out dead plants from last year. Under the leaves were new sprouts of crocuses and daffodils that were poking through the earth. When she finished clearing out the dead stuff she concentrated on planting new life. She bought many colorful bedding plants, flowering shrubs, and miniature ornamental trees and when she finished, she surrounded the perimeter of the garden with a low black wrought iron ornamental fence to offset it from the lawn.

She contracted a local artist to design a plaque to place in the garden when she was finished. Looking around, she was proud of what she'd accomplished on her own. She had worked diligently getting her garden the way she wanted it. Although she had not spent time there while her mother was alive, she was making up for it now. This was her garden, and she was claiming it as such. Looking over the entire garden, she searched for the perfect spot for her plaque. Picking up the stake with the sign on it, she hammered it deep into the ground. Before leaving to go into the house, she took another long look around and there in the middle of the garden, among all her beautiful plants, flowers and shrubs stood her sign that read...

Garden of Eden

4

On a warm sunny spring day, Eden was sitting in her garden with a book. With every intention of reading it, but thoughts of her mother crept in again. Getting up, she strolled around and touched her fresh spring flowers and plants while remembering that her mother had also spent time out here. It still saddened her that her mother had never once invited her to join her. She hadn't asked for her help in the slightest way or invited her to be a part of this beauty. She had always been here alone, and Eden could not remember one time that she'd spent in the garden while her mother was alive. *'What a sad thing to remember,'* she thought, *'having a beautiful garden such as this, and she hadn't wanted to share it with anyone, especially her daughter.'* While her mother had been here in her garden alone, Eden spent equal amounts of time on the beach just as alone as her mother was. Giving her head a brief shake, she tried to rid herself of the unpleasant memories. There were no hopes now of mother and daughter moments, their time had passed.

Early spring still held several hours of sunshine but became chilly towards the end of the afternoon. Sitting back down on the swing, she'd hoped to enjoy the last bit of warmth before the temperature dropped and forced her inside. Picking the book up off the swing, she held it on her lap unopened. Dropping her head back and closing her eyes, she exposed herself, for a few glorious moments, to sun on her face. Opening her eyes again she raised her head and sat absorbed in watching a butterfly flitting about from flower to flower as it explored the plants. A smile spread across her face as she enjoyed the beauty and remembered the endless hours of work that she now appreciated. She loved her garden, and she was enjoying the fruits of her labor.

As she watched the butterfly, a voice broke the silence and frightened her.

"Hello there!"

Springing to her feet, Eden inhaled deeply and clutched her throat as her heart hammered wildly in her chest.

"I'm so sorry," a voice said from out of nowhere, "I didn't mean to startle you,"

Her hand was fluttering on her throat as she tried to compose herself. Her eyes focused on the voice of the stranger who stood next to her fence.

"I saw you sitting there many times and wanted to say hello and introduce myself to you. I'm Luke" he said, holding out his hand to her, "Luke Roman." I moved in next door a few months ago. Still off her game and frozen with fear, she looked at his hand, back up to his face again and he smiled at her shyness. Stepping closer, she felt uncomfortable that his hand was still extended toward her, so she reached out and put her hand in his.

"Eden," was all she said.

He nodded toward her sign and said, "So the garden is named after you then?" Wearing a broad and friendly smile, he was the picture of handsomeness. He knew he had her when he mentioned her garden.

"Yes, it is," she croaked with a dry mouth and throat. Her only male companion had been San, and it seemed to be enough for her since she'd had no real experience with boys or men over the years. Yet, here stood this very handsome man, not more than a few feet away from her. He had snapping brown eyes that made her heart leap every time she dared to look into them. She could not believe the attraction she felt toward this perfect stranger! *'What was it about him that drew her to him?'* she wondered. *'Obviously, he must have felt the same way, or he wouldn't have been watching her for months.'* Trying not to stammer she said, "I didn't know anyone had moved in next door, the place has been vacant for years."

"I bought it a several years ago," he said, "but I wasn't in a position to move here till recently. I've been here long enough to see you put the garden together though and may I say, it's quite lovely."

"Thank you," she said lowering her head again feeling shy from his compliment and obviously quite proud of her accomplishment.

She was not used to having a conversation with males, except for San. She had lots of contact with women when they brought sewing for her to mend, but as far as men went, there had only San Taman. Conversations with San were easy, this was not.

"You're very beautiful Eden," he said, knowing he had her attention.

Blushing, she smiled shyly and said, "Thank you, Luke." Looking down, she saw that he was still holding her hand and she slowly pulled it away. "It was nice to meet you, Luke," she said, turning to go back to her swing.

"Would you like to have dinner with me," he blurted out, hoping she'd respond. So... we can become better acquainted... as neighbors?" he stammered, trying to stall her.

Stopping abruptly, she turned to look into his brown eyes and hesitated for only a brief moment. She didn't know why but she smiled and said, "Yes, Luke, I would like that."

"Great, is seven ok?"

"Seven it is, I'll see you then." Smiling at him, one last time, she wandered back to her swing. As she sat down, she could not help but wonder about what she has just agreed to. *"I've not been on a date in my life!"* she thought nervously. She asked the age-old question that every woman in the world asked themselves in this same situation... *"What am I going to wear?"*

~

It was time to start getting ready, and she went in to have a bath. She didn't realize how nerve wrecking this dating business was. For her first date, she chose a lovely knee-length black dress and black wedge heeled sandals. She chose a cream cashmere shawl and a black clutch for her keys and a tissue. Deciding to wear her hair down, she thought it would be a nice change from her usual ponytail. Checking herself several times in the full-length mirror, she tried to convince herself that she looked ok.

Promptly at 7 o'clock, Luke rang the doorbell. When Eden opened the door, he was not surprised at what he saw. He'd noticed her beauty many times over the past several months, and this was no exception. Mostly, when he saw her, she had either been in her garden or walking the beach. He'd taken notice that she had continuously been alone. He'd had a much better view of the beach from his property than she did. There were times when he watched her at length as she bent over to pick up things off the beach, but he was too far away to see what it was. He'd thought she might be a rock collector and from time to time, he'd seen her stop for several minutes as if she were waiting for someone. He'd watch her for a several minutes, and it looked as if she was in conversation with another person, yet she was always alone. After a little while, she'd turn and go home. He'd always wondered where that little bag came from? He had not seen it while she was beachcombing, but she always had it on her way home. Maybe it had been something she had carried for her rock collection...?

His thoughts wondered came back to her, "You look absolutely beautiful tonight, Eden."

"Thank you," she said shyly. She hadn't had much if any, practice in this sort of thing and it was difficult to graciously accept compliments without feeling a bit embarrassed. Her one wish was that she'd get through the evening without embarrassing herself or him. Luke was the only person who'd ever told her she was beautiful.

"Are you ready?"

"Yes," she said, "as soon as I get my wrap." Coming back with the cashmere shawl, she wrapped it around her shoulders. Her clutch bag was tucked just under her elbow containing only a tissue and her house key.

Luke had wined and dined Eden until she felt dizzy and lightheaded. She hadn't had much involvement with drinking either, like most of her life experiences. The dinner wine he'd chosen was smooth and bubbly, so she had several glasses, and by dessert, Eden began to feel very strange. Feeling light-headed and dizzy, she asked Luke to please take her home.

Walking her to her door, she was having difficulty focusing on getting her house key out of her bag. Dropping it several times, Luke finally asked if she needed help. Passing him her bag, she reeled on the steps. She giggled a few times before he found the key to let her in. Opening the door, she stumbled across the threshold, and Luke caught her before she fell. While balancing her, he closed the door with the toe of his shoe while keeping her steady. Resting her head on his shoulder, she closed her eyes. Hearing her door slam shut, she flinched, picked her head up and opened her eyes. Finding her manners, she wanted to thank him for dinner and say good night. Looking into his eyes, her heart began to beat rapidly, and she forgot what it was that she'd wanted to say. Gazing into each other's eyes, he kissed her, and she didn't try to stop him. Her very first kiss. Although she was enjoying it, she had absolutely no control over her body or her emotions. She remembered several thoughts going around and around in her head as she tried her best to focus. '*What is happening to me? What are these feelings? What am I doing? What is he doing?*' Suddenly everything seemed puzzling, and she couldn't think clearly. She sensed that he had swept her up in his arms and was carrying her somewhere... but where? She felt her body being laid down, but she didn't know where. She could not open her eyes to focus on anything in the room, and her head was swimming in a sea of confusion. Then, she vaguely caught sight of her trunk and realized she was upstairs in her bedroom... *'I'm in my room, I'm home, and I'm safe,'* she thought, and that was all she remembered until she woke up the next morning with a pounding headache.

5

Eden, barely making it into the bathroom, fell to her knees and hugged the toilet bowl. She was in agony as she made several attempts to recall her night out with Luke but could not. *'What happened and how did she get to her room?'* she thought. Assuming it was safe to get up off the floor, she washed her face, brushed her teeth and started back to bed when something caught her eye and stopped her mid-stride. Through blurred eyes, she saw something draped over her trunk. Squinting from a pounding head, she picked it up. "A necktie? A necktie?" she asked herself twice. Stumbling backwards, her heel came down on a sharp object, and she wobbled slightly to get past it before it pierced her foot. Carefully she bent down to pick it up. Looking at it strangely, she recognized that it was a studded cufflink that belonged to Luke. *'What were those items doing in her bedroom?'* *'What had happened here last night?'* she wondered.

Holding the tie and stud, she sat down on the bed and tried to recall some of the events of night before. Raising her eyes to the ceiling, she was at a total loss for memory. Lowering her head, she saw it... blood... on her sheet. The reality of what must have happened turned her stomach upside down. Rushing back to the bathroom, she dropped to her knees and wondered when this nightmare was going to end. Picking herself up off the floor for the second time in only a few minutes, she was beginning to feel weak and ragged. Leaning over the sink, she splashed cool water onto her face. Pressing a towel against her face for a few seconds, she brushed her teeth again then went out to face the mess. Feeling sick and dizzy, she began to panic. Fear stabbed at her gut as she realized that Luke must have raped her! The proof was right there on her bed! The sobering truth was, he had raped her while she was unconscious!

Shakily, she picked up the phone to call the police and for someone to pick up. After reporting the incident, her thoughts, from the night before, had come back to haunt her. She remembered thinking that she'd hoped she wouldn't do anything to embarrass herself or Luke. Although this had been her first experience with date, she felt that if this was the result, she wanted no part of it again.

Scanning her room for more evidence to give to the police, she waited for them to arrive. Noticing the trunk, her heart dropped while thinking the worst. She'd always kept it locked, and she forced herself to go and check it. Pulling on the handle, relief swept over her... it did not open. *'Thank God!'* she thought as she went looking into her hiding place for the skeleton key. Opening it, she lifted the quilt that covered the coins and saw that everything was still there. Laying the quilt back over the money, she closed and locked the trunk. Putting the key back in its secret place, she heard the doorbell ring. Wrapping a robe around herself, she went to answer it. Nervously opening the door, she greeted two officers. Stepping aside, she invited the male and a female in. A feeling of de ja vu swept over her. Leading them upstairs, one officer searched the room, gathered up and bagged the sheet and Luke's two items for evidence. Eden and the female officer went into the bathroom to collect samples from Eden. When the samples were taken and secured in plastic containers, the officer assured her that she was free to either shower or bath. She'd also told her that they would be in touch with her as soon as there was anything to report. Going downstairs, she showed them out and bolted the door. She'd never, in all the years living there, felt a need to double lock her doors. Climbing back up the stairs, she felt tears stinging her eyelids.

Sinking into a tub of hot water, feeling sick, abused and alone, she put her head back on the edge of the tub and cried until her tears were gone. The water was nearly cold when she finally stepped out. *'How could she ever wash away the shame she'd felt,'* she wondered. After drying herself off, she quickly brushed her hair without looking at herself in the mirror. Exhausted from the trauma, she put fresh linens on her bed. Shamefully, she pulled the thick drapes together and crawled in. Sleep came easily in the darkened room, and it was a blessing.

Standing in the shadows, not far from her bed, there was a silhouette. Watching her close her eyes, San stepped out from the shadows and watched her while she slept... Sensing she was being watched, she bolted upright out of a half sleep. Feeling a little lightheaded, from drinking, being sick and not eating, dizziness set in momentarily. The room was in darkness, but she saw a silhouette... then she heard his soothing voice...

"It's ok Little One," he whispered. And the sound of his voice calmed her immediately as she fixed her eyes on him. He was just sitting there, on her trunk. The shadow his face, but she sensed that he was deeply saddened.

"San, are you ok? How did you get in?" she asked without realizing what a stupid question that was.

"I'm sorry I wasn't here sooner Little One," he said as he rose to his feet and came close to her bedside. "You won't have to worry about Luke ever again, now close your eyes and go back to sleep."

"San, how do you know about Luke?"

"I know about Luke, Little One," was all he said.

"San?" she said in a quivering voice.

"Yes, Little One, I'm here, go back to sleep."

Closing her eyes as he'd asked, she drifted into a peaceful sleep. San couldn't resist the opportunity as he gently wiped a strand of hair from her face and laid his hand gently on her cheek. Lightly touching his lips on her forehead, he sat back down on her trunk and watched her as she slept. Even though she was asleep, she could hear San's voice, far off in the distance, speaking to her and as if in a dream, she could hear his words.

"Don't worry Little One, Luke has been taken care of. When you wake up in the morning, you will feel a sense of relief and your fears of seeing him again will be gone. I will always be here with you and Adam. She felt a light touch of his lips brush her forehead, and before sleep had fully enveloped her, she thought about what she'd heard. *'Adam...? Adam? Who is Adam?'*

~

Weeks had passed, and Eden had been out taking her daily walk along the beach. Luke rarely entered her thoughts, and she felt relieved that she had not seen or heard from him. Feeling as though she had not been completely traumatized about the rape, she was happy to be moving forward with a peaceful mind. The fact that she was raped would be with her for a long time, and

41

she was determined to let go of her one night with Luke. Mistake made but lesson learned.

Earlier than usual, Eden was out and about for a morning walk. While walking, she couldn't help but notice what a gorgeously, warm and sunny day it was turning out to be, so early in the season. Suddenly, a strange and chilling feeling began to creep over her. At first, she thought it must be the sun, but it was way too early in the morning for the sun to have such a harsh effect. *'Had she eaten enough breakfast?'* she wondered. *'Could that have been it?'* She hadn't fell hungry when she started out and wondered if she'd eaten enough to sustain her on her walk. Feeling perspiration forming on her forehead, she wiped her brow with her hankie. Her entire body felt drenched with sweat, and her stomach began to feel unsettled and queasy. Feeling frighteningly weak, she sat down on a large rock before her legs gave out from under her. Sitting down, she put her head between her knees trying to figure out what was happening to her. Wanting to crawl off somewhere, she just wanted to sleep this off whatever it was, but she had to make her way back home. Raising her head, she felt dizzy, and her eyes weren't focusing as she pondered how far she'd walked. *'How was she ever going to make it back home feeling this weak?'* she wondered.

Beginning to panic, Eden realized she was farther down the beach than she'd originally thought and doubted she'd find the strength to make it back. *'I'm going to close my eyes for a few minutes,'* she thought, *'just long enough to gather enough strength to get up and move.'* Closing her eyes, she felt as if she was airborne and was being swept away. The strangest thing was, she could not open her eyes to see where she was. She kept asking herself the same question as she glided through the air,

'What is wrong with me?' She was scared, yet she had a complete feeling of safety as if something had taken control over her body. Somewhere far off in the distance, she heard San's voice again...

"I said I would take care of you and Adam, Little One... and I will..."

'Adam? There was that name again...'

Waking up on her bed, Eden was covered with a soft and lightweight pink throw that she kept on her trunk. She didn't know how she got there, but she was so thankful she had made it home... Lying there fully awake now and still not feeling up to par, she made a mental note to call her doctor in the next morning and hoped maybe she would shed some light on this. She had to know what had happened to her out there on the beach. She thought it might be a touch of flu perhaps, but why did it hit her so hard and so fast? She began to wonder, 'Was she eating right or eating enough. Did she need more rest, a vitamin supplement perhaps?' She was not going to panic unless she had reason to. She would wait for the results of her checkup before hitting the panic button.

Arriving a few minutes early for her appointment, Eden tried to relax before her name was called. Finally, she was taken into one of the examining rooms to wait while her doctor finished with other patients. When the doctor opened the door to see Eden, they made small talk for a few minutes. They exchanged a few pleasantries, talked about the weather and got past the usual chit-chat. Although her physician knew her quite well, Eden was in worse shape than she had ever seen her. She had always come in for routine check-ups and was all around a very healthy gal.

She got around to the reason why Eden by asking the usual questions. She began by asking her how she was feeling, and Eden described in detail about the event on the beach the day before and was careful to leave out the part about how she managed to get home. The doctor insisted on a full examination since it was nearly time for her yearly pap test.

About ten minutes into the examination, she had the answers to all of Eden's questions.

"Eden, you're pregnant!" she said, smiling at Eden and waiting for her reaction.

Her brow furrowed as if she had heard wrong. "What?" the word stumbled out. The info she just heard was not sinking in.

"You're going to have a baby, Eden," she repeated.

"I am?" Her mind jumped instantly to Luke.

"Yes, you are, and I'd estimate that you are probably eight or nine weeks along, but we'll know more when we do an ultrasound."

"When can we do the ultrasound?" Eden asked. "Right now," she answered, "If you have time."

"Yes! I have time!" she said excitedly. Passing Eden a gown, she showed her to the dressing room while she prepared the ultrasound equipment. Nervously, she came out of the stall wearing her hospital gown. Instructing her, the doctor told her to get back up on the table, and she would be with her shortly. She chatted idly with Eden giving her a few details of what she was going to do.

44

Raising a tube up for Eden to see, she explained, "This is going to feel cool," as she squirted a jelly-like substance on her tummy. "Ready?"

Nodding with excitement as the doctor placed the instrument on her tummy, she instantly heard, *'Boop - Boop' 'Boop - Boop.'*

"It's a heartbeat!" Eden said wide-eyed.

Asking if she could see her baby, Eden admitted that she wasn't certain what she was looking at. She pointed out to Eden where the baby was and traced the outline of the image with her finger. "This is it right here," she said, "and I'd say, by looking at this, your due date is going to be right around Christmas, how exciting!"

"A Christmas baby?" Eden was amazed at what she was seeing and hearing.

With a mischievous grin, the doctor said, "We can do another ultrasound in a about another seven or eight few weeks if you'd like to know what it is?"

"You can tell, that soon?" she asked.

"Yes, I will book you in for an appointment in a couple of months!"

~

Arriving on time for her appointment, Eden was excited to know if the sex of her baby would be detected.

45

Settling in on the table and with a much larger belly, she waited for the doctor to come in.

The door opened, and Eden smiled broadly. "Are you sure this will work?" she asked.

"Yes, of course, it will, Eden, are you certain you'd like to know?"

Looking at her doctor for only a few seconds, she broke into a smile and nodded.

"Then let's get started," she said with a grin. Connecting the machine, she brought it closer to the bed and lifted Eden's gown up over her tummy. Squirting on the gel, she began to roll the probe slowly over her stomach. Eden could hear the heartbeat again, and as she watched the screen, nothing made sense. *'Boop–Boop' 'Boop-Boop'*

"Where is the baby?" she asked, feeling confused.

Touching the screen, she traced the image again for Eden. "Right there," she said, "are you sure you want to know?" she asked again for certainty.

"Yes, I do," she said, smiling.

"It's a boy, Eden," she whispered softly as she looked into her patient's eyes.

A familiar voice came into Eden's head as she heard the words, *"I'll take care of you and Adam."* Focusing on the monitor with fascination, one word escaped her lips... "Adam?"

~

Once Eden had become aware of her condition, she wanted to make her trips to the beach shorter, but she still wanted to try to walk every day. She certainly did not want a repeat of the time she fell ill out there. Being four months along, she opted to wear looser clothing. Her plan was to walk the beach more for the exercise than profit. Choosing to pick up her treasures, if she saw any, but certainly not as often. Seeing San on her outing, he inquired as to how she was feeling and asked if she had had any other weak moments on her walks. It was only then that she realized it had been San who'd gotten her home.

"San," she began as if it was normal, "I'm having a baby and it's a boy." He was the first one she'd told, and it was as easy as breathing to her. She was happy to be able to confide in him.

"Yes, Little One, I know."

As if a light had clicked on, she looked at him, smiled, and said, "Yes, of course, you do, you knew about Adam before I did." San just looked at her and nodded. Looking intensely into his eyes, she heard the words resonating in her head again, *'I will take care of you and Adam.'* He knew exactly what she was going to say. Shading her eyes, she glanced down the beach. Searching for something to say, she turned back to tell him that she was heading home and to thank him for helping her, but San was gone.

6

Eden felt it was the right time to open her trunk. She had made several trips to the bank for coin wrappers but did not do anything with them. She was ready to start the process. She counted out a thousand dollars in coins and wrapped them up in the appropriate amounts. When she had finish wrapping up several rolls, she would take them to the bank. For each one thousand dollar lot, she requested a one thousand dollar bill in return. Then she would bring the bill home and place it inside the small chest she had used for her treasure money when she first started her collection. This was going to be a long process, but she had to keep at it until the trunk was empty. She wrapped coins after her daily walk until her back was aching, and she felt it was long enough.

The small box was filling up with one thousand-dollar bills, and it was much easier to store them than all the coins. Each day the trunk contents lowered as she wrapped and wrapped. She never had company except for the ladies who still brought sewing for her, but that was not very often. The staff at the bank never questioned where she got the money. It was as if she were bringing a twenty-dollar bill in for them to cash in for smaller bills. No one seemed to notice how much she brought in and they just filled her requests and continued to serve other customers.

Eden breezed through summer and fall and was having bouts of nervousness if she spent too much time thinking about the baby. Some days she could not wait for Adam to be born and other days it was a scary thought. She got through the last two holidays before Christmas. Then she began to decorate her house and a few weeks before Christmas she brought out her small artificial tree and trimmed it to finish off her decorating. She never had a real tree, but now that she would have a child this time next year, she was considering having one.

Eden woke up Christmas Eve morning with uncomfortable cramps and lower back pains. It stayed with her for most of the day, so she decided to call her doctor at home to tell her what was happening. Her doctor had long since given her the house number in case of an emergency. She felt this was not an emergency as much as it was to find out what to do next.

"Can you get yourself to the hospital, Eden?"

She told her she was sure she could and got several items together in a small bag and called a cab. She heard the taxi driver blow the horn alerting her of his arrival. She went outside, locked her door and went down the steps to the sidewalk. Just as she was about to seat herself in the cab something caught her eye. She turned and saw San standing on the same spot, leaning against the lamp post, as he did when she was a child. Only now he was facing in the opposite direction since the canal was behind him instead of in front. She knew she was the only one who could see him so instead of waving she just smiled at him. Smiling back, he gave a 'thumbs up' gesture as she lowered herself into the backseat of the cab. Before she could get the door closed and look up again, he was gone.

It was well into the evening, and Eden was in a lot of pain. Nurses kept coming in to check on her, but she was not dilating enough to go into the delivery room. She asked if her doctor was there yet and they assured her she would be when they were

49

ready for her. This was taking longer than she thought it would and she wondered why she'd come to the hospital so soon.

"Why is it taking so long?" she asked, but the only response she got was, "Babies come when they're ready for the world." And she was left alone again.

She rang the bell for a nurse to tell her something had just happened, and when they examined her, they told her that her water had broken, and it was time to go. Her pains were almost unbearable at this point, and she glanced up at the clock on her way down the hall; it was 11:55 p.m. She saw her doctor as soon as she was wheeled into delivery and relief swept over her.

"Are you ready Eden?"

"Oh, yes, I am and so is this baby," she said, as she grimaced with pain.

The delivery went well, and without complications and before long, it was all over.

At 12:05 a.m. her Christmas baby was born. When they laid him in her arms, she looked him over with pride and noticed how absolutely beautiful and perfectly formed he was. With tears of joy mixed with exhaustion, she pulled him close and kissed the top of his head and whispered, "Merry Christmas, Adam." As they wheeled her out of the delivery room, she thought she saw a figure standing in the shadows... no, it can't be... but as she lifted her head to get a better look, there he was, smiling from ear to ear and looking as if he were the proud dad. As she was being wheeled into her room, she held her baby close to her body and silently wished he was, indeed, her baby's father.

~

Adam truly was the love of her life. He was a beautiful, healthy, happy and good-natured little guy and he was a joy to have around. He had the same snapping brown eyes which had gotten her into trouble in the first place, and he had an unruly crop of brownish blond hair, but Eden rarely thought about Luke anymore. Although she'd had his son, he was still just Adam. He would likely grow up to be the image of Luke and equally as handsome, but he was just Adam... She knew he'd would never be Luke's son... he was her son. She refused to give Luke any more credit than that. He may be Adam's father, but it ended there. He'd made a mess that she was left to clean up and Adam is her son and Luke would never be anything more than a distant, ugly and unpleasant memory to her. She had never laid eyes on him again. Sometimes she wondered why his house was closed up and always in darkness, but she just figured it was the coward in him and that he'd high-tailed it out of town before she awakened the next morning and realize what had happened to her. But his house was still there as a constant reminder of the way he treated her. She thought she might have handled it better had it been a one-night stand with no intention of contact the next day, because she guessed that was what a one-night stand meant, but this was cruel and ugly. At least he was gone and if she had her way he would soon be forgotten. Once she had gotten those thoughts out of her system, she rarely thought about him again. Somewhere in the back of her mind, she had laid him to rest as if he had died and she was moving on.

~

Adam was growing in leaps and bounds, and Eden loved being with him. He was absolutely no trouble at all. He rarely got sick, except for the common cold, and hardly ever cried even during teething time. He took everything in its stride and was very patient. Many times, Eden would go upstairs to his room, which was directly across from hers, to check on him. There San would be, sitting as if on guard, just watching him sleep or rocking him in the rocker that sat in the middle of the floor. Sometimes she would just stand in the doorway and watch as he held Adam and she could tell how much he loved him. Other times she would tiptoe in, and they would chat in whispers, so as not waken him but mostly she would let San have his private time with him. The only time he could be with him like this was when he was asleep, and Eden knew it was his special time. She was always happy to see him in the nursery but as morning approached he was nowhere to be found but she knew he was there somewhere.

It seemed no time at all when Adam had learned how to pull himself up on the furniture and tried to put words together. They spent their free time playing in The Garden of Eden. They would sit for a few minutes on the swing while Eden held on to his shirt tail so he wouldn't topple off. She enjoyed walking around with him and pointing out all the different flowers and letting him touch and smell each variety. He loved the colorful butterflies flitting about, and he would try to catch them when they landed near him on a flower. She took pictures of him near her plaque, only a small part of the hundreds she'd already taken.

Now and then she went back in time and thought of how much she had missed not being a part of this garden with her mother. It was something that she did not dwell on for too long anymore and felt it was better left in the past. Nothing could change what happened, so it was best left alone. She was making beautiful memories with her son now, and what was important, it was right here and right now, in the present, not the past. It was absolutely wonderful to be able to share her garden with her son.

Adam's favorite place was Eden's garden. He loved to play there whenever possible, which was almost every day that it was warm enough to go outside. Eden still felt the presence of San all around her. She did not have to see him or hear him. She just sensed that he was somewhere close by and all she had to do was bring him to mind, and somehow, he appeared.

On her trips to the beach, with Adam, she often caught sight of someone out of the corner of her eye. She never made it obvious that she knew he was there; he simply wanted to stay at a distance and on 'guard.' Sometimes he was visible to her, so she'd know he was there and other times he would watch over them in silence. This was one of the reasons why she never felt alone. He watched over Adam as if he were a precious gemstone and he watched over Eden as he had since she was a small child, silently considering her his Gem.

7

Adam was growing up so fast, and soon he'd be ready for kindergarten. Eden wondered where the time had gone. He was also getting more and more independent with each day. Eden was happy to know that he had inherited her love for the outdoors. He especially loved to walk on the beach. Surprisingly enough he did not do too badly walking on the stones. She expected him to stumble since parts of the beach were not always sandy and smooth. When they'd reach a sandy area though, Adam would try and capture seagulls by chasing them across the beach. He'd insist they bring bread along to feed them on their walks. He was happy no matter where he was, and he made Eden happy just being around him. They both loved the same things which included long walks, playtime at the beach and in the garden and all the pretty things that grew there. They could be found in either of these two places well into the fall and all they needed to enjoy it, was a nice warm sweater.

~

One Christmas, on the spur of the moment, Eden bought Adam a doctor's bag. It was a gift from 'Santa Claus,' and she would never forget the joy he got from it. Oh, how he loved his doctor's kit! It was the one thing he played with at every opportunity. Showing him how to use the stethoscope, she put the ends into his ears while placing the other end on her chest. After listening to her heartbeat, he pressed it against his own heart and heard his own. Then he had turned his attention to his teddy bears and used the stethoscope on them and gave them pretend medicine, wrapped them in bandages or put multiple band-aids on them when he thought they had a boo boo. He was so proud to be a 'doctor.' "I'm going to be a doctor when I grow up mommy," he told her in a rather serious and determined voice. Reassuring him, she said when he grew up he could become anything he wished to be, and the possibilities were endless. Money would never be an issue. She could put him through medical school ten times over if that was what he wanted. He never changed his mind.

When the next few Christmases rolled around, he asked for gifts he could use in his room such as lab kits and anything medical or doctor related. He developed such a fascination for the medical profession that it became first and foremost in his mind. When he was further along in school, he wanted a library card, and he only brought home medical journals and books that were related to doctors, medicines, breakthrough discoveries, anything that would help him absorb as much as possible. He was very bright, a fast learner and made excellent marks in school.

Adam was a loner just like mother, and he did not mind being at home. He kept busy helping her in the garden, reading books while she did certain gardening tasks, or he would work on projects for school, but he was never bored. He never asked for much and never wanted money although Eden gave him some for his pocket. He was happy and content to do his own thing. It seemed he was happy just to be home with his mother and she never considered him a mama's boy. She guessed it stemmed from their close relationship that had developed over the years. After all, it was just the two of them and had been since the day he was born. He never knew about San, so most of his time was spent with Eden.

55

~

With graduation rolling around, Adam began applying to local universities in his last year, and he was accepted at every school where he applied. He had made straight 'A's' all through school, and he was an ambitious, bright, and handsome young man. Eden was so very proud of him. He had been moving towards his goal since he opened that first doctor's bag. That little black bag is what had kept him focused and had inspired him to do what he loved. It still sat on the shelf in his closet, and every night San still visited his room after he'd fallen asleep...

Adam chose the university closest to 56 Garden Place since he didn't want to be away from home during his first years in university. He would have to leave home soon enough and felt this was not the time. The hospital, where he was born, had already offered him his residency when he finished his studies and he'd accepted. He whizzed through at the top of his class, aced every course he took and could not wait for the hands-on experience to begin.

Finally, the day came to begin working at the hospital. He was there only a few weeks when he was paged to answer a call. Picking up the phone, the doctor said he was unable to make it to the hospital on time and asked Adam if he could assist in a delivery. He reassured him he would be there as soon as he could but wanted Adam to take over the case until then.

"Are you ok with that doctor?" he asked.

"Yes Sir, I am." Adam could not have been any more excited as he made his way to the delivery room. He was going to deliver his first baby!!!!

8

Sarah Matthews was not only pregnant, but she was also alone. Neither the pregnancy nor being alone had been part of her plan, but here she was, and she had no choice but to deal with it. When she had met Peter Jacobson, she knew he had no interest in marriage or responsibility of any kind. She had known and accepted the agreement from the time they started dating, and it was her choice too. When they moved in together, that was how it stayed, no expectation of any kind from either of them. Everything was running quite smoothly until she told Peter she was pregnant. This was the beginning of the end of the relationship as it started on its downhill slide. They certainly had not planned the pregnancy, and when they learned from the first ultrasound that she was carrying twins, Peter freaked. She knew he was not 'dad' material and she had no intention of raising another child, which was exactly how he acted most of the time, afraid of growing up. He'd never wanted children, but neither had she, at least not yet anyway, and like everything else, nothing is foolproof, not even their birth control. But now it was what it was, and she was pregnant.

Sarah had felt for months that Peter had been changing, and she didn't like what the change was doing to him or her and their relationship. Living with the tension between them was horrible. His mood swings and lifestyle were too stressful for her and her unborn babies. One night he'd gone out, and as usual, he'd forgotten to come home for dinner. When he did return, she knew this was no longer what she wanted. At first, she thought of giving him an ultimatum, but she already knew the result that would bring. He certainly would never take the 'either,' and she already knew he would most definitely take the 'or.' Finally, she gave him the option to leave, and she didn't have to ask him twice. She helped him pack up what few things he had, and they said goodbye. She felt a sense of relief as he drove away. Watching the last bit of taillights disappear into his dusty wake, she could not even shed a tear.

She spent the next several months preparing for her babies' arrival. Living stress-free without Peter acting up at any given time was helping her to appreciate what she had. Even the thoughts of having to raise two babies didn't scare her, and as the birthing time neared she was actually happy, she was alone.

~

Sarah met Adam at the hospital after being told he'd be assisting with the delivery of her babies until her doctor arrived.

Above his mask, she saw a beautiful pair of snapping brown eyes, and she knew at that very moment she'd had lost her heart.

Looking at her, he said, "Hello Sarah, I'm Dr. Thomas and I'm here to help until your doctor arrives, how are you feeling?"

"It's nice to meet you, Dr. Thomas," she panted, "I'm in quite a bit of pain right now, but I guess that's why we're here." She thought a bit of conversation might help but it didn't, and she was trying extremely hard not to scream out in pain.

Adam guided her through at every turn, and the births actually went well.

Back in her room, Sarah waited for her babies. She thought about the delivery room, which hadn't been bad at all, and the handsome young doctor. He had introduced himself, but for the life of her, she could not remember his name. By the time he'd gotten into the delivery room, things started happening fast, and there was no time for remembering names. She was told her doctor was running late and another doctor would be in to assist, and now she was wondering if she would ever see him again or would her own doctor return to the case. Once rounds began and it was her turn, it was Adam who entered her room. It was all coming back to her now as she remembered those snapping brown eyes, brownish blond hair that was not necessarily neatly combed, and a smile that showed beautiful and even white teeth. He stood about six feet tall but from where she was lying he looked even taller, and she could not help but notice how extremely handsome he was. Then her next thought was, she was having a hospital crush, and she had to get over herself.

"Ready to go home tomorrow, Mrs. Matthews?" he said with a smile.

"Tomorrow? So soon?"

"Is there a problem?"

"Ms. Matthews," she corrected him, "but please call me Sarah and yes, there is a problem, but its only nerve related."

"How so?"

60

'Just like a doctor,' she thought, *'short and to the point.'* "I'm a little nervous going home with two newborn babies knowing I'm all they have to depend on and it's freaking me out just a little."

"Where's the dad?"

"I have no idea where he is, he wasn't dad material, so we agreed it was best that he leave. I've had no contact with him since the night he left, and that's the end of that story. I'm sorry," she said shyly, "but I've forgotten your name."

"Dr. Thomas, Adam Thomas." It was as if it was the first time he really saw Sarah. He noticed they were approximately the same age and she was very pretty. He also saw how nervous she was and tried to calm her down a bit. "My mom is a single parent, and she did ok."

"She is? Are you an only child?"

"Yes, I am, and we made out just fine. She was and is an awesome mother, and you will be too. She was both mom and dad to me, and I didn't know what it was like to miss something I never had. And you know something else, I've always felt as if I was being watched over when mom wasn't around, and it made me feel safe. I never knew who my dad was and never had a need to ask. To be honest, I don't particularly care to know either, it's not that important to me. He wasn't there for me while I was growing up, but 'someone' always was and still is. It's like I have a guardian angel, I guess." Adam didn't know where all this was coming from and surprised even himself when he said it. He never mentioned his Angel to anyone nor talked about it with his mother or anyone else for that matter.

He didn't know Sarah very well at all, and yet he felt a familiar presence with her.

Just then a nurse wheeled in double bassinettes on a baby cart. Adam looked at Sarah and saw her face light up, and it made him smile. *'Gosh,'* he thought, *'she has a nice smile.'* The twins were only a few hours old, but they were as cute as anything he had ever seen lying there in their individual beds, fast asleep. He could not stop himself from asking, "Have you chosen names for the babies yet?"

"Yes, I have," she said, "I'm naming them Jacob and Eve."

"Really?"

"Yes, really," she smiled, "why so surprised?"

He smiled at her and suddenly, he got a strange urgency to tell her. "My mother's name is Eden, mine is Adam, my mother named her flower garden, 'The Garden of Eden,' he said, putting his fingers up in air quotes, and I do know that my father's name is Luke." Pausing briefly, he continued, "You... are Sarah, and you're saying we now have Jacob and Eve, doesn't that sound a bit strange to you? Should we build an Ark?"

They both laughed and looked at each other for a few seconds and then slowly shifted their eyes to the babies. The four of them, alone in the room and it felt almost as if they were all a part of his family. There was that familiar feeling creeping in again, and Adam looked around the room to see who else was there. No one was, of course, that he could see, but San was standing over the bassinettes watching the babies just as he had done with Adam all those years ago. Adam sat down on Sarah's bed just like he belonged there.

"This is weird," he said.

"What's weird?"

"I feel like 'my Angel' is here with us," he said. Seconds later Adam felt a light touch on his shoulders, and a peaceful, familiar feeling swept over him.

Adam asked Sarah's permission to hold one of the babies, and she nodded. Picking up Jacob, he laid him in her arms, and for the second time, their eyes met and held for a brief moment. Turning away, he went over to the pink bassinette and picked up Eve and sat in a chair near Sarah's bed. Sarah watched as he stared at the tiny pink bundle in his arms. San smiled at the sight he was witnessing and as he smiled at them, so did Adam and Sarah... at each other. They were becoming a family! A family that Adam wanted! The only other thing he had wanted this badly, was to become a doctor, and if that had not happened, he would not be here with Sarah.

San stood behind Adam's chair, looking down at Eve, just as she opened her eyes for the very first time. She did not look at Adam... but was focused on something above him and she looked straight into San's eyes, smiled at him and closed her eyes again. For a moment Adam wondered if Eve could actually see someone there with them. That was when Adam knew they were not alone in the room. Sarah had not noticed anything because she was busy with Jacob. Adam was used to his Angel by now and whoever it was; it never seemed to leave him. He smiled to himself as he felt a tiny breeze pass by him to affirm his thoughts.

~

Sarah had taken her babies home early the next morning as soon as her own doctor released her. She was disappointed that she hadn't seen Adam one more time, but maybe that was a good thing. Why get close to someone if they were never going to be in your life. Then why was she missing him so...? She consciously pushed Adam to the back of her mind so that she could carry on with the tasks at hand. She had two babies to care for, and she had no time to dwell on the impossible dream. She was not as afraid as she thought she would be and how she loved her two little angels. Her thoughts crept back to Adam a few times as she remembered him holding Eve in her room but forced the thoughts away to concentrate on her life in the moment... which was right here and right now with her babies.

9

Adam was disappointed when he finished his morning rounds and went to Sarah's room, but she had already left. He felt a sense of loss not seeing the bassinettes in the room.

'Why do they allow mothers to go home so soon after giving birth, anyway?' he fumed. *'Well, I could go on like this for days, but the fact remains she's gone home!'* He didn't realize he had been talking aloud and to himself! Pacing back and forth a few times, he rubbed his chin, left the room and went down the hall to the elevators. Pressing the first-floor button, he waited for the ride to end. When the doors opened, he went straight to the records department and asked the clerk for Sarah Matthews' file folder and waited. Bringing back his request, he thanked her and headed for the cafeteria for a cup of coffee. Sitting down at a far end table, he laid the folder down. Taking his pad and pen from his jacket pocket, he opened the file and copied down the info. 123 Sheppard's Way and her phone number was there as well, so he wrote both down on his pad. Closing the file and finishing his coffee, he took the folder back to the Records Dept and thanked the clerk again for her time.

Now that he had this information, what was he going to do with it? Would she think he was insane if he called her for no reason? He couldn't come up with a reasonable excuse to pick up the phone. Why did he want to call her anyway? He really did not have to ask himself why... he just wanted to see her again plain and simple. He paced around the room a few more times and then made a decision.

"Hello?" he heard her say.

"Sarah?" he asked... *'That was dumb, who else would it be...!'* he thought.

"Yes, this is she."

"Sarah, this is Adam."

She had no idea what to say. Then, opening her mouth, she said, "Doctor Adam?" She felt herself blush and felt rather embarrassed and she waited for him to hang up on her.

He laughed and said, "Yes, it's Doctor Adam."

"Hi!" she said her heart racing, "How are you?"

"I'd be better if you'd allow me to come over."

"Here?"

He laughed again, "Do you have a problem with that or am I being too forward?"

"No, I don't have a problem with it, I'm just surprised, I guess."

"Well?"

"Well, what?"

"May I come over?" he asked again, smiling to himself.

"Oh yes, I'm sorry, I guess I'm a little rattled, yes, yes, come over, do you have my address?"

"I do indeed, I got it from your file, and I'll see you shortly."

66

Sarah was an absolute mess! She didn't know what Adam wanted or even if something was wrong. She didn't have answers, so she decided just to wait for him. In the meanwhile, she raced to the bathroom to freshen up and comb her hair before he arrived. Both babies were down for their naps, and when she thought she looked presentable enough, she went outside to wait for him.

Her heart leapt when she heard a car slow down and saw the signal light come on. Pulling up in a small silver car, he turned the engine off and got out. Sarah stood up to greet him. He was smiling as he walked toward her. "Hello, Sarah."

"Hi, Adam, is everything ok?"

"Yes, why?"

Standing in her driveway, they faced each other as Adam and Sarah, not doctor and patient. Looking into his eyes she knew there was no problem, he was there to see her! Taking a chance, a brave chance, he pulled her into his arms for a hug. He was smiling when she hugged him back. There was no need for words right now. He pulled back far enough to look into her eyes, and without much thought, he kissed her, lightly at first, and when she didn't resist, he put a little more passion into it but not enough to scare her. He pulled away from her to look into her eyes.

"What's going on Adam?"

"I don't know Sarah, I honestly don't know, but what I do know is that I wanted to see you again and something urged me to come over."

"I'm glad you did because when I left the hospital, I didn't think I would ever see you again."

Standing next to Adam's car, looking very pleased with himself... San.

Adam had taken a leap of faith when he decided to call Sarah. It turned out to be one of the best decisions he'd ever made. He was deeply in love with her, and he absolutely adored her twins as though they were his own. He knew for certain that he wanted them to be his family. They had spent every possible moment together since he made that first call and neither one was surprised at the progress they were making in the relationship. They were devoted to each other, happy to spend every moment together and were deeply in love. He had always been thankful that he had been chosen for Sarah's delivery.

That day had been the turning point in Adam's life. He knew Sarah was the one when he spent time in the hospital room with her and the twins. A few months into the relationship, he talked to his mother about her. He wanted to bring her home to meet her. Eden was surprised since he had not mentioned a lady friend before and now she was curious. This gal had to be special because from what she remembered he never had time for girlfriends and never talked about dating anyone either.

"Yes Adam, I'd like to meet your friend."

"There's something else I should tell you too, mom."

"What is it Adam?" she asked with curiosity.

"Sarah has twin babies."

Eden was about to furrow her eyebrows in question when she noticed San sitting quietly looking at her and nodding his head in approval.

"Well, I think that's wonderful Adam, please do bring her and the babies over."

Smiling, she knew if San approved it must be a good thing.

When Adam mentioned the meeting to Sarah, she was a bit reluctant at first. She didn't know what Adam's mother would think of her being a single mom with two babies. But, she remembered Adam telling her that his mother was a single parent as well. Feeling a little less nervous, she realized they had something in common.

~

"Mom, I'd like for you to meet Sarah and these are her twins, Jacob and Eve. Sarah, I'd like for you to meet my mother, Eden."

"It's very nice to meet you Eden and thank you so much for inviting me to your lovely home."

"It's nice to meet you, too, Sarah and thank you for coming, please come in and sit down so I can get a peek at these babies." She smiled at them as they slept and told Sarah how beautiful both babies were. She looked up in time to see San again, standing quietly by smiling at Eden and nodding his approval again and Eden gave a slight smile to herself. Adam noticed a glance between his mother and who...? There was no one else there... or was there? Just as the thought came into his head, he

69

felt that familiar brush on his shoulder, and he glanced down to where he felt the brush and smiled to himself. As San passed by him, Eden saw Adam smile. Eden was used to having San pop in and out, and it was familiar to her. With Adam though, he only had the familiar feeling that he never talked about and never questioned it... ever.

~

Adam and Sarah had been seeing each other for five months, and that was long enough for him. When he decided to asked Sarah to marry him, she was thrilled! Knowing they were meant to be together, they had no reason to wait. The sooner, the better is how they both felt, and Adam could not wait to have them as his family and begin proceedings to adopt the children.

They arranged a dinner with Eden so that they could tell her their news. They didn't want to get a babysitter, so they took the twins along, too. Adam finally told his mother that he asked Sarah to marry him and that she'd accepted. Eden was not too surprised with the news because she already knew how much Sarah and her babies meant to her son. Smiling, Eden got up from the table and walked over to Sarah and opened her arms to her. Sarah stood up, and they hugged each other warmly then she walked over to Adam and hugged him.

He whispered, "Thank you, Mom," and they smiled at each other.

Returning to her chair, Eden raised her glass. "Welcome to our family Sarah and of course, Jacob and Eve as well, I'm so happy for you both, congratulations!" Touching their glasses together,

70

they took a sip to end the toast. They thanked Eden for the toast and the congratulations and told her they were not planning to have a long engagement.

Since Sarah did not have family of her own, she asked Eden if she'd help her plan the wedding. Eden told her she would be more than happy to lend a hand and anything she could do she just had to ask. She then asked Sarah if she would consider having the ceremony in the 'Garden of Eden' and she was thrilled when she accepted. Eden not only wanted to help plan the wedding, but she asked Sarah if she would be offended if she paid for it as well. Stunned, Sarah didn't know what to say. She never expected Eden to pay for her wedding, but Eden had insisted that she wanted to, as 'part' of their wedding gift. Sarah graciously accepted her offer with a hug.

"Part?" Sarah asked, "what does that mean?"

"No more question, my Dear, we have a wedding to plan and since the house is plenty big enough, would you consider having the reception here as well? This old place has a ballroom that has not had its doors opened in years and it's time they were, what do you say?"

"A ballroom? I never would have guessed. I'd love it!"

Eden explained that she'd lived there her entire life. "And," she said, "as a matter of fact, I was born and raised in this house. After my parents died, it became mine, and then I made it into a home for us," she said pointing between herself and Adam. "It's an enormous house, and not much of it has been used over the years." She looked at Sarah for a few minutes without speaking.

Sarah noticed her silence and asked her if she was ok and she assured her she was.

"Would you and Adam consider living here after you are married and making this your home too?" Sarah furrowed her eyebrows as if to question what she just heard.

"Well, I just asked if you'd like to live here Sarah," she said with a smile. Wrapping her arms around Eden, she hugged her tightly. "Oh Eden, I absolutely love it here! And this will make the perfect place for the children to grow up in as you did and then Adam. I would love to live here if it's what Adam wants as well."

Eden smiled and told her they would ask him before any other decisions were made. At dinner that night, the subject about living arrangements was brought up, and Eden asked Adam if he would like to move his new family in after they were married. Adam was quite surprised that his mother would offer such a generous gift. She had lived there for so long with no one to bother her. She was always able to do her own thing without second thoughts, but now she was willing to share her home, not only with him but his new wife and two children. He was overwhelmed by her generosity and told her just that. And, so it was decided, by all concerned, they would all be living at 56 Garden Place.

Eden saw to it that Adam and Sarah had the most wonderful, perfectly beautiful wedding day and she spared no expense. Everyone that had been invited arrived in plenty of time to mix and mingle around the garden. Sarah invited friends she had for years, and Adam invited his hospital friends and colleagues. The weather cooperated, the sun was glorious, and everyone had a fantastic time. The ceremony went beautifully, and Adam and Sarah had chosen to write their own vows, and it was a touching few moments between them.

During the reception, Eden took both Adam and Sarah aside and asked them to please follow her to the garden. Once outside Adam turned to his mother and asked if she was alright.

"Yes Adam, I'm fine," she said with a mischievous grin.

"What are you up to now, Mother?"

She was hiding something behind her back which is why Adam questioned her playfully. She brought an envelope out from behind her back and handed it to them. "This is the other part of your wedding gift."

Adam took the envelope and looked questioningly from the envelope to her and then flipped open the flap and pulled out two airline tickets to Paris, France, for their honeymoon.

Sarah was stunned! "What! Paris? Eden!!" She put her hand over her mouth in total disbelief and tears sprung to her eyes.

Eden walked over to her, put her arms around her and held her while she cried tears of joy. "You make my son happy, Sarah, and that means the world to me," she told her while she cried. "Now, dry those tears and open your other gift."

"What other gift? This is our gift," she stressed as she held out the tickets.

Eden handed her another envelope and Sarah stared down at it like it was a foreign object. "Here you go Sweetheart; this is for you and Adam."

She took the envelope and slowly opened it up and took out several layers of one thousand dollar bills! She spread them open with a flick of her fingers and counted ten of them and looked back at Eden with her mouth open in disbelief.

"That's for you and Adam to spend on your honeymoon or however you want to, it's yours to do with as you please." Sarah was crying again and was overwhelmed by Eden's generous gifts to her and Adam.

"Come on now," she cooed in a soft, loving voice. "We'll have none of that on your wedding day, you are my daughter now Sarah, and the gifts I've given to you are only a small part of what is to come!"

Neither she nor Adam knew what she was talking about and they didn't ask. They were both too stunned by what had just happened to think about anything else. Eden mentioned she would like to have the babies with her while they were away if it was ok with them. She told them they may as well get adjusted to their new home now as later. Sarah thought the whole thing was just a dream and she was floating on her own cloud. They were not over the shock of all this when Eden asked them to please follow her.

"I'd like to show you both something, please come with me."

They went up to the second floor and stopped at the bedroom that was Adam's for so many years. She opened the door, and they both gasped at what they saw.

"Mom, this is great, when did you have time to do all this?"

"I didn't, I hired a decorator." She'd had the decorator redo Adam's room into a nursery for the twins. Since he spent most of his time at the hospital or with Sarah, there was plenty of time to get it done. It was beautifully done, and there was everything in it that any two children would ever want or need including the wallpaper, paint, curtains, rocking chairs, toys, and two cribs. Eve's crib was painted white, and Jacob's was done in wood. The one in wood had been Adam's when he was a baby, and she'd had it refinished for Jacob. The room was done to perfection, right down to the babies asleep in their cribs and a nanny watching them while the reception was going on downstairs.

"Mom!" Adam said, "it's lovely, and we love it, thank you so much for doing this and making this into the babies' room. It's comforting somehow knowing it's the room that I spent so many years in."

"You're both welcome, now come with me."

They went up another flight of stair to the third floor, and Eden opened the door and stood back and swept her hand through the air indicating for them to go inside. Entering the room, they saw the most beautifully decorated honeymoon suite that was fit for a king and queen!

"Everything you'll need is here, food and drinks and everything is under control downstairs, the twins are being looked after, and I will see to the guests. Your plane doesn't leave till tomorrow night, and you can fill me in on the babies' needs tomorrow before you leave. So, enjoy your wedding night! I love you both." Blowing them a kiss, she softly closed the door and returned to the ballroom.

Adam and Sarah could not believe the lengths that Eden had gone through to give them this wedding night. There was unlimited champagne in a medium size fridge, a fruit basket, a plate with several kinds of cheese with bread and crackers and ice cream in the freezer if they so wished. Looking around the room, the king size bed was quite intimidating to them both.

Sarah walked over to the bed, and there was the most beautiful pale pink silk and lace ensemble she had ever seen. Turning, she looked shyly at Adam and picked up the ensemble and walked toward him. When she got in front of him, she touched his face, looked at him and smiled playfully and turned with her back to him and asked if he would unzip her wedding dress. Adam's hands were not quite as steady as he would have liked them to be, but he managed to pull the zipper down without getting it caught. When Sarah felt it reach the bottom, she thanked him and walked away into the magnificent en-suite to change for him.

As much time as they had spent together and as much in love as they were, they had respected each other. They had resisted temptation and waited for this very night. Pouring them each a glass of champagne, he sipped his slowly as he waited for the en-suite door to open. He had admitted to no one, not even Sarah that this would be his first time being with a woman, and at this

76

very moment, waiting for Sarah to come out of the dressing room, he was especially glad he had waited.

Adam never felt the need to go out and chase down prospects for one-night stands. He watched his friends did that, only to brag about it the next day to their buddies. He'd never seen the point to it. Maybe it was because he felt like he was being watched or there was a presence with him all or most of the time that kept him on the straight and narrow. He was not sure, but, at this very moment, whoever it was he was glad for the presence. He smiled to himself at the thought, but little did he know that San has been watching over him almost constantly and right now he was one floor below in the nursery where he had spent so much time watching over Adam. Now San had everyone he cared about all here under one roof, and he was pleased. He so loved these babies, especially Eve when she smiled at him with those beautiful eyes.

~

Adam had been in deep thought when the click of the door handle brought him back. He looked up just as Sarah opened the bathroom door and walked out to meet her husband. Adam could barely catch his breath, from her beauty. Taking a few steps to meet her, he took her instantly in his arms and was completely overwhelmed at how much he loved his bride.

The newlyweds were up early the next morning so they would have lots of time with everyone before leaving for the airport. Sarah had been so excited she could not sleep and had laid awake most of the night thinking about how much she loved Adam and this night would bond them even more. It surprised her that she was the first for Adam and so honored that he saved himself for her. She felt totally blessed. The day went by faster than they expected it to and the twins slept through most of it and, so not to upset their routine, she let them sleep.

They thanked Eden many times for allowing them to have this wonderful honeymoon. She said she was happy to do it and wished them a great time. They were all packed and ready to leave for the airport, said their goodbyes and kissed the babies, as they waited for the cab to pull up.

10

When everyone was ready to say their goodbyes, San had popped in for one last look at the happy couple before they left. Eden was the only one who knew he was there, of course, and she was careful not to glance at him while the family was around. Just as Adam picked up one of the suitcases, he felt a brush against his shoulder, and he stood stark still for a few seconds. Eden had seen the look on his face and walked over to him.

"It's ok Adam," she said in a whisper while nodding her head to reassure him. She so wished she could tell him about San, but her childhood promise made it impossible. He heard a tone in his mother's voice just then, and he figured she knew more about this than he had expected her to. Yet, there was that time when he'd caught her smiling, back when he'd felt the touch of his guardian angel. Adam had begun to think his mother could see this presence of his... what? ...Angel?

"Mom?" he whispered, pulling her aside, "Can you see someone else here with us?"

She glanced up at San, with pleading eyes, for the answer because she did not want to lie to her son. San nodded his approval, so she whispered, "Yes, I can."

"Then can you tell me if it's male or female?" he whispered back.

She looked at San again to be certain she was not betraying him, and he smiled and nodded again. "Male," was all she said, and

Adam knew that was all he was going to get out of her, for this time anyway.

"Mom, this guy... feeling... has been with me since I can remember. Having him in my life has filled the void of not having a father, it's like he is my father," he stressed. This was one of a very few times that Adam had ever mentioned the word 'father' to her. She hugged him tightly and looked up at San again, thanking him with her eyes. Seeing pride on his face, San knew that Adam had felt him watching over him all these years and that he had considered him fatherly. Before today it was all guesswork on Adam's part, and now he finally knew the truth and secretly he was glad he was not imagining it this entire time.

"Thanks, Mom," he said glancing around the room one more time... hoping maybe to see someone too. His eyes fell onto a framed photo on the mantle, and when it moved slightly, he knew that was where he was. Smiling in that direction, Adam still saw nothing.

Sarah had broken the spell by asking Adam if he was ready to go and told him the cab was honking for them. They were out the door and into the cab waving and blowing kisses to Eden as they drove off. When she went into the house to look for San, as usual, he was nowhere to be seen. She had felt relieved that she was able to put Adam's mind at peace.

Adam had wondered for so many years about this presence but had not asked questions in case people would think he was losing his mind. Sarah had listened to his story when they met in the hospital room, but she never gave it much thought afterward. Being pleased that he was even in her room, she let him talk just so that she could listen to the sound of his voice.

She hadn't cared that he was carrying a ghost around in his pocket, she would have listened to almost anything he had to say at that point. She loved the sound of his voice, and he could have had all the little idiosyncrasies he wanted, she did not care... he loved her, and she loved him, and that was all that mattered... Adam and her babies.

~

Eden had taken the twins out to her garden every day. They either slept in the fresh air and sunshine, or she would spread a blanket on the grass so they could roll around while she sat and watched them trying to play. Either way, she adored being with them. What fun it was to have little ones around again. *'There hadn't been anyone 'small' around her house since Adam,'* she thought. She was extremely happy that Adam and Sarah had agreed to live there with her. The days and nights would not be so long now that she had these two little ones to occupy her time. She spent her waking hours feeding, bathing, playing, rocking them to sleep, singing lullabies or reading stories. She had learned how to manipulate two baby slings, one for the front and one for the back for beach walks. They were still small enough and not too heavy for her to handle carrying them both. When the tide was in, she'd take them in their double stroller and walked everywhere and nowhere, in particular, just to be out in the fresh air.

While Adam and Sarah were in Paris, she had called the Nanny in to sit with the babies. She needed to take care of some personal business at the bank. Once she had decided on what she was going to do, she wanted to get it done, and it was something she was not going to put it off any longer. Getting out her box of money, she counted out what she wanted and put the box back inside the trunk that was at the foot of her bed. It seemed that no matter how much money she took out of that box it never made the slightest dent in the stacks. From the time she had spent rolling the coins and taking them in for large bills, she had never really known exactly how much money she had. She didn't really care, she knew she had enough and that was the important thing and the amount never mattered to her.

Eden left for the bank to do her business as soon as the Nanny arrived. She explained to the Nanny that the children were asleep, and she'd hoped to be back before they woke up.

Waiting for her turn at the wicket, she thought about why she was there. She wanted to set up two new accounts for the twins to start college funds for them. While at the wicket, she opened each account with five thousand dollars. Once a month she planned to make a trip back to make deposits into each account. Knowing that Adam didn't make a lot of money as an intern and Sarah was a stay at home mom, Eden wanted to take care of her grandchildren. She had enough money to take the burden off them, and she enjoyed being their providers until they could do it on their own. And, she did it with a lot of love, grace, and generosity.

She'd made the decision to secretly keep the bank books in her trunk after she made each monthly deposit. As the twins grew so would their bank accounts, and no one would be the wiser except Eden and San, of course... San knew everything. She would know when the time was right to expose her secret. Until then, the bank books would remain her secret.

Adam and Sarah had been honeymooning for just over a week and would soon be home so Eden enjoyed every minute she could with Jacob and Eve. She had decided, shortly after the honeymooners left for Paris that she was going to 're name' Jacob and call him Jake as a shorter version because she thought 'Jacob' sounded too grown up for him right then. She would deal with the consequences later when Sarah got back, but for the time being, he was going to be Jake to her.

On the day Adam and Sarah were due home Eden spent the day preparing for their arrival. She baked and cleaned and had Jake and Eve all decked out in new outfits and looking quite precious. Having difficulty keeping them awake, she finally took them upstairs to their cribs. She was thrilled they were living with her. She loved those two little angels with all of her heart. Finally, and right on time, the cab honked out front and Eden ran to the door to greet the newlyweds. Sarah looked happy, tanned and absolutely worn out while Adam had gotten his second wind napping on the plane. "Hi!" Eden said and waved from the front door as they got out of the cab.

Sarah had run up the steps to hug Eden. She was excitedly talking about everything at once that Eden motioned for her to slow down so she could understand what she was saying. Eden left the door open while Adam paid the cabbie and collected the bags from the sidewalk. It was wonderful to see them both, and she was happy the trip went well and that they were home safe and sound.

"How are the babies, Mom?" Sarah asked with excitement and Eden looked at her rather strangely.

"Mom?" Eden asked, with a smile and raised eyebrows.

"I'd like to call you. Mom, if you don't mind."

She went over to hug Sarah. "Mind? I love it!"

"I'd really like to go up and see Jacob and Eve before we do anything else, I've really missed them."

Before she could get away, Eden stopped her, to tell her what she had done with the name change. "I hope you don't mind Sarah, but I've been calling him Jake for two weeks, is that ok or should I stop now?" Sarah spoke the name aloud, not necessarily to anyone in particular, just to herself like she was trying it out.

"Jake," she pondered aloud, "Mom! How cute is that?! I think it suits him, don't you?"

"Yes, I do indeed."

Sarah went up to the nursery to see the babies, and she could not believe how much they had grown in just two weeks! Both were playing in their cribs and as happy as could be. She thought Eden had taken very good care of them.

11

Weeks turned into months, and the twins had been walking and spending time with Eden in her garden. They loved it out there with 'G-Ma' as they so fondly called her. 'G-Ma' was easier to say than grandma or grandmother when you are still learning how to put words together.

Adam had long since adopted them, and with Eden's help with lawyer fees, it happened even sooner. She had wanted them to be legally her 'family' as much as Adam and Sarah did and more importantly, she had wanted these Little Ones to be her grandchildren, the sooner, the better and that is how it went.

By the time the twins were a little over a year and a half old they were two going concerns. They were talking almost in full sentences and with Eden reading to them every day they were becoming experts on story books. Jake was a little bigger in size than his sister which was normal for boys to grow faster than girls. Eve was just a little thing no bigger than a minute but every bit as smart as Jake and just as rough and tough as her brother. She learned how to handle herself very early on, and Jake knew it.

~

The twins started daycare in the Fall and in doing so they had other playmates of the same age. They'd only had each other to play with and had no other friends their age. Everyone agreed that daycare would be a great experience for both of them. Soon they would be in regular school, but they still had the summers to play on the beach with their G-Ma. They were quite fast and steady on their feet, and they raced each other up and down the sandy shores of Kanyon Beach until they flopped breathlessly on Eden's blanket to rest up. Once they had rested, they were ready to build sand castles and play in the sunshine. They were two very happy and well-adjusted loving children, and Eden loved them with all of her heart. In those days Eden would often help them build their castles, but there were days when they were independent spirits and wanted to make their own so G-Ma could decide who had done the better job. Even though Eve's was usually neater and more solid and well done, she didn't have the heart to choose between the two. They both tried equally as hard to impress her and so the choice had remained that they were both so wonderfully done that she could not possibly decide who's was best. There were never hurt feelings, and they were happy with her choice.

The twins were too smart for daycare. They had learned so much from Eden that at three years of age they were both ready for kindergarten. Sarah was impressed with how much time, patience and love Eden had put in with the twins, and it was plain to see that she regarded them as her own grandchildren. She couldn't have loved them any more than if they had been Adam's children. Daycare had been a boring adventure for them both, but they enjoyed the company of the other children.

~

Time and Tide waits for no man, and the same was true with the twins. They had been enrolled in kindergarten and daycare had become a distant but pleasant memory for them both. When it was still warm enough for beachcombing and playtime, Eden often took them out to give them a bit of fresh air after being at school all day. On one of those days, when the twins returned from school, they changed into their beach clothes, had a snack and a glass of milk and then they headed out for an hour or so of recreation before supper. On that particular day, Sarah decided to tag along with them and get a little sunshine herself. The kids played as they always had while Eden and Sarah chatted idly back and forth. They had been on the beach close to an hour when Sarah felt she'd had enough sun. She decided to go back to the house and Eden agreed that she would go with her and get supper started.

Eve wanted to stay a little longer and begged them to please let her. Eden was not concerned about her being there alone from her own experience as a child playing there. She told her she could stay but warned her again about the tide, telling her when she saw the tide coming she must get back to the house in plenty of time because the water came in really fast. Eve promised just a few minutes longer, and she would be home, so Eden and Sarah had gone back to the house without her.

Eden was in the kitchen preparing vegetables and Sarah was helping as much as she could, but mostly she was just there to keep Eden company. While they were casually chatting, Eden had kept a close eye on the water from the window over the kitchen sink. She was not able to see a lot, but the beach was visible in patches, and she could also see the water. She wanted to make certain the kids were safe. Then in an opening, she caught a glimpse of Eve running back to the house. She had blown in through the front door and yelled for Eden, asking where she was.

"G-Ma, where are you?" she screamed nearly out of breath with excitement. Raising her voice enough to tell her she was in the kitchen, Eve came running to her.

"G-Ma! Look what I found! I found these treasures on the beach and look at all the pretty colors! I washed and cleaned them off too G-Ma, look how pretty they are!"

Sarah looked at Eve as if she had grown two heads and could not believe what all the excitement was about. "Eve, honey, those are just pieces of broken glass." And with that statement, she got up, patted Eve on the head and left the room.

"Show me what you have there, Little One."

She opened her tiny fist and showed her. Eden's face lit up in a smile.

"These are beautiful Eve! Are you sure you got them on my beach?"

"Yes, G-Ma, right out there around the corner," she said pointing toward the canal, "on my way back here."

Eden's thoughts went back to Sarah and wondered why she had seen only broken pieces of glass when it was plain to see these were beautiful pieces of gemstones! Just then, San Taman's voice had crept into her mind, and she heard his words. "You must not tell anyone about me until you are really sure they have your gift." Eden's heart had given a sudden leap when she realized what was happening right here in her kitchen. She pulled Eve close to her and gave her a big warm hug and kissed the top of her head. Eve had her gift! She became overjoyed knowing that. Although she was not biologically related to her, she had the gift!

She looked at Eve and said, "Little One, I want you to go back outside and wait for a man called San Taman."

"Santa Man?"

"No, Little One, listen carefully to me, Sweetheart, San Ta man." She said slowly so she could hear the pronunciation of his name. He will buy your treasures from you and then you can bring your coins here to me. I will have a box ready for you to put them in, ok?"

Eve nodded her head not really sure what she was agreeing to but knew she trusted G-Ma with all of her heart.

"Eve, do you think you can keep this secret, this is a 'gift,' Little One, and no one except you, me and San Taman can see these beautiful treasures, that is why your mommy thought they were broken pieces of glass. Eve listened closely to Eden as she spoke. While she explained about San and the treasures, she thought to herself that she had been approximately the same age as Eve when she first experienced her gift and had her first encounters with San. She knew how overwhelmed her young granddaughter would be, so she had decided on another approach. She picked her up and sat her down on the kitchen counter, so they were basically the same height. She put her index finger under Eve's chin and turned her face toward her, so she could look into her eyes as she spoke.

"Eve, honey you must listen to me and listen very carefully, ok?"

Eve nodded her head and Eden began to tell her about her first encounter with the treasure.

"When I was a little girl, about your age, I found treasures in the same place where you found yours today. When San Taman approached me to buy my treasures, he told me I could not tell anyone about him until I was absolutely certain I knew they had my gift, and I never told anyone until today. That was quite a few years ago, and no one ever knew about my treasures or the coins he gave me for them or about San. It is a secret I have kept all these years, and it has not really been that difficult either."

"What does San look like G-Ma?"

Eden had described him as best she could, and Eve's face lit up in a big beautiful smile when she heard it.

"I know who he is G-Ma!!"

"You do?"

"Yes, G-Ma, he plays with me in my room, and I see him all the time watching Jake and me while we play on the beach. Just today he told me the tide was coming and I should tell Jake it was time for us to go home, and G-Ma, when I'm afraid of the dark, he rocks me in the chair in my room. Jake doesn't see him, but I do. I used to see him when Daddy rocked me too. He was always just standing there with us, but I don't think Daddy could see him either. Is he magic G-Ma?"

"No, honey, he isn't magic, but he has been with me for a long time, and no, daddy cannot see him, but he watches over him, too. He's kind of like a Guardian Angel I guess, and I don't consider Angels as magical. Angels are from Heaven and magic is not. I've been told that magic is more of the Devil's playground than Heavenly."

Eden had always known there was something special about Eve and until that day she had not known just exactly what it was. It is like when you are trying to remember someone's name or the name of a certain tune that's bouncing around in your head, but you can't quite grasp it, and then it's gone. It was nice to be able to share San with someone, and she was especially glad it was Eve since they were so close. She had not minded keeping San a secret all those years, and she had not been able to stress enough just how important it was for her to keep the secret, too. "Do you understand, Eve, what it means to keep a secret?"

"I think I do G-Ma, a secret means only we know, and we can't tell anyone else what we know, isn't that right G-Ma?"

She was overwhelmed with love for this child as she gave her a big hug and kissed the top of her head again. "Yes, Eve, that's exactly what it means, and you must be very careful around Jake and your friends that you don't tell them by mistake." Eve had heard everything that G-Ma had said and waited for her to finish before she spoke.

"Whenever San is around he puts his finger to his lips, and I never feel like I want to tell anyone that he's there, that's why I thought he was magic. I like him G-Ma, do you?"

"Yes, I do Eve, and I don't think he would still be here if I had told our secret, so in order for us to keep San around, we must honor his wishes. I must tell you, Eve, it isn't right for me to ask you to keep secrets, especially at your age when we are teaching you life lessons about truth, honesty, and trust. Not to justify this as the right thing to do, but in truth, we aren't keeping secrets by trying to hide something we've done; we're keeping it as a request from someone who needs us to. Does that make sense to you, Eve?"

"Yes it does, G-Ma, and it's not a bad thing because we didn't do anything bad that we are trying to hide. G-Ma, I never knew his name, he never told me. He spent lots of time with me, and he knew my name, but I just called him Magic man."

Eden smiled as Eve told her story, in the childlike way she spoke, and the way she emphasized and expressed herself with hand gestures. She was still a tiny thing, and Eden sometimes had forgotten that she was just a little girl. They had so many grown-up conversations from the time Eve first learned to put sentences together; she was a very intelligent little girl. She had missed them both when they started kindergarten. She had filled her days with projects and hobbies, but she watched the clock and waited for them to return home. When they had started regular school, once again, she had to fill those long, lonely hours while they were away.

"G-Ma?"

Her voice startled Eden and brought her back from her daydream.

"Um?" Eve said while pulling at Eden's arm.

"G-Ma?"

"Yes Honey, what it is?" she asked as she followed her gaze.

"Hi, Little Ones," he said as he appeared there with them.

"Hi San, how are you?"

He did not answer her question he just looked at Eve with that friendly smile that was so familiar to her.

"Would you show me your treasures, Little One?"

She looked at Eden with a surprised look on her face as if to make certain it was ok to talk to him. Eden nodded and told her it was ok, and that he would buy her treasures as they had discussed earlier. She told Eve she would be right back and left the room. Eve looked up at the Magic man, who now had a name, 'San Taman,' and reached into her pocket and brought out her treasures. She opened her hand so he could see what she had found. At that very moment, it took him back to when Eden stood in front of him with treasures in her palm.

"My, my Little One, these are very beautiful!"

Smiling up at him, she nodded her head in agreement.

Looking at her, his mind trailed off again to another place and time. It was back in the hospital room on the day she was born. Adam was rocking her, while he visited with Sarah, and she opened her eyes and looked straight at him. San was thinking about baby Eve and Eve was having her own moments in time when he played with her in her room or when she saw him at the beach, but San's voice broke the silence for both of them.

"Would you like to sell them to me?"

Feeling comfortable with him, it was like she had always known him, and San's voice brought her back to the moment.

"Yes, I would San."

And in the meanwhile, Eden was busy in her trunk looking for her first money box for Eve. When she had found it, she took it downstairs to the kitchen. Giving it to her, Eve opened it and handed over her treasures to San while he, in turn, had placed her coins inside the box. Closing the box, she passed it back to Eden.

San looked at Eve and reminded her about the secret that the three of them shared and asked her if she understood what it was all about.

"G-Ma explained it to me San Taman, and I'll keep our secret."

"So, when you find more treasures you'll keep them for me?"

Smiling up at him, she said, "Yes, I will San Taman, I'll keep them for you."

12

It had been a long time since Adam had been able to spend any quality time with Sarah and the twins. His residency demanded long hours, and usually, he was on-call even when he did get home. Although he missed his family, he loved what he was doing at the hospital. He was an excellent doctor and, to those he provided treatment for, they had a great deal of respect for him. He had become a pro at delivering babies since he'd first taken over for Sarah's doctor and he wanted to learn every aspect of the medical profession before choosing his specialty. He'd put requests in at every available department necessary to assist him in a chosen field. It had been a long and difficult decision for him to make since he loved it all, but still, a decision had to be made. Leaning toward maternity, he was not certain if it had been the thrill of delivering his first babies or the fact that it had been his first big, unassisted medical case. Whatever it was, every birth from then on had given him the same thrill of helping bring a new life into the world. He was still torn, though, because he also loved being in the ER and he's proven it by being at the hospital for twelve to fourteen-hour shifts and sometimes even longer, depending on the day. He was in his element with the trauma, the hustle, the snap decisions he'd had to make with every emergency situation, and it made his day when he got through it without losing a patient. He was not there to lose patients he was there to help heal and fix them.

Being proud of his accomplishments, Sarah tried not to allow his long hours get to her. She was glad she and the twins had been there with Eden and not living somewhere on their own. If she'd had to go through those years alone, she would have been quite lonely from missing Adam. Eden had been a Godsend when she asked them to move in with her. The house was always busy, and the kids spent most of their free time with G-Ma. Being a wonderful grandmother, Eden always found time to be with them. She'd spend hours with them whether it was inside the house, out in the garden or on the beach.

From out of nowhere, Sarah remembered the pieces of beach glass that Eve had brought home and wondered why Eden had made such a big deal over them? They were pieces of broken glass but being the delightful G-Ma that she was, she had made every piece special to Eve. Yet, she couldn't decide whether or not it was a good idea for Eden to allow her to believe that it was more than what they were. She was only a little girl, at an impressionable young age, and even little girls can be disappointed. Sarah was off on a trail of different thoughts and remembered that Eden even had the Eve talking to herself. Sarah had noticed Eve chatting with an invisible friend from time to time, and she thought that could not be a good thing, yet she read somewhere that most kids conger up imaginary friends. She had seen Eve talking up a storm in her room sitting in her rocking chair and then from the third-floor bedroom window she had seen her talking to this imaginary friend of hers as she played on the beach while looking for broken glass.

Eden was not her biological grandparent so she could not have inherited it from her, but she had noticed that she talked to herself a lot, too. Deciding to mention her concerns to Eden, she found her in the garden and went out to join her.

"Hi Sarah," Eden said when she saw her walking towards her. "Come and join me and enjoy the sunshine while we talk."

"That's why I'm here Mom. I'd like to talk to you. I'm beginning to have a few concerns about Eve."

"Why Sarah? What are you concerned about?"

"I've noticed on many occasions that Eve is talking to herself and has these conversations with people who aren't there."

"We are never really alone Sarah, and most kids her age have imaginary friends and Eve is no different." She could hardly explain San to her, and she could not very well tell her that he was Eve's constant companion as he had always been with Adam and all of them, for that matter. The only difference was, Eve could see him, Adam knew about him, but she was not sure if Jake knew about him since he had never mentioned anything to her.

Eden wondered why it was only Eve who could see San Taman and Jake could not. They spent most of their time playing together, being the only two children in the house. She had spent as much, if not more, with them as Sarah had, yet Eve and San seemed to have found time to be alone and connect. And not only that but Eve also inherited Eden's gift and yet they were not blood-related. She had no idea how the gift was passed on, then again, she didn't know where she had gotten it either! She was thrilled that Eve had the gift and that she was able to help her with the treasures and take care of her coins for her. She had been able to deposit them into her college account. She had long since put a plan in motion to deposit the same amount in Jake's account that went into Eve's. San was always there with coins for Eve's treasures, and Eden saw every piece she found and was as excited about them as she had been when she'd found her own.

97

Jake was not left out of anything, he was a good-natured little boy, and he loved his sister like all brothers do, but he had not always been willing to beach comb with her. She was constantly looking for and picking up broken pieces of glass, and he had not seen the point in tagging along for that. He wanted to look for shells, dead crabs, periwinkles and all the good stuff since he didn't care about broken glass. He had his sand pail and shovel to look for things and then carry what he'd had found back home in his pail. He showed everyone all the treasures he'd found, and each piece had a story. They listened to him run through his time on the beach, and he'd become a great storyteller.

He always loved being with G-Ma, but he also loved being alone on the beach to do his own searches. There was never any indignation in his thoughts as he justified that every piece was as precious to him as Eve's old pieces of broken glass were to her.

Eve had been busy treasure hunting and hadn't noticed that Jake had wonder off when he thought he had found all there was to find in that area. He had decided to venture a little farther down to a section of beach he had not been to before. Once he got there, he found more than he thought possible and some of it he had not seen on his part of the beach. Being excited and happy to find all these different seashells, he'd lost all track of time, and as he piled his treasures into his sand pail and concentrated on his findings, the tide was coming in...

By the time he'd realized where he was, how long it had taken him to get there and the time it would take to get back, he knew the canal would be almost at high tide. Starting to panic, he didn't know what he was going to do. There was no way for him to get home! His mind going in so many different directions, nothing was making any sense to him. G-Ma had warned him and Eve so many times, over and over again, to be home before the tide came up. *'Oh, he was in so much trouble,'* he had thought, as he sat down on a piece of driftwood. Not being able to contain his tears any longer, he laid his forehead on his crossed arms over his lap and began to cry. He was out there all alone on an unfamiliar part of the beach, where he was not supposed to be, and the water was coming up to high tide and had kept him from running home to safety. Frightened, he shook from head to foot. There was nobody around to help him. He lifted his head and scanned frantically up and down the beach, but there was no one around, and he cried even harder. To make matters worse, nobody knew where he was, so how would they find him? As far as they knew he could be anywhere.

Standing up, he ventured farther up to the top of the beach as he watched the tide creeping higher and higher. The worst part was, he didn't know exactly how high the water rose. There had been no place for him to go and the water was right behind him! He was up on the beach as far as he could go but he didn't know if the water rose up the cliff or not, so he continued to search for an escape route. He noticed a tree that had uprooted from bank erosion. He grabbed on to a branch and climbed up and sat on a bough and prayed it would hold him. Sitting there, he hung on for dear life. In no time at all, the tide had already covered the spot he'd just been. Once again G-Ma's words came back to haunt him, as he remembered her telling them how fast the tide can come in. He had begun to wonder how long he'd have to sit there. Knowing enough about the tides to know, he knew it took hours for it to go out and he had figure if he waited a few hours it would be down enough that he could touch ground again and get himself home. He had never been so full of panic in all his young life. Putting his head down on the branch, he began to cry again. He needed his mommy and daddy so badly right then.

Little did he know that mommy and daddy had already been alerted by Eden that it had gotten late, and Jake had not come home. She had begun to worry about her brother. Eve had gone home and told G-Ma that she could not find Jake. She first thought he must have gone home when she realized it was time to leave and he was not with her. She told them she had called and called for him, but he hadn't answer, so she'd assumed he had left for home. Everyone had begun searching, phone calls were made to friends' homes, and no one had seen him. All the playgrounds and parks where he sometimes played were searched, and there had been no sign of him. The canal had filled up, so they could not search the beach, and since Eve said he wasn't there, they had to search elsewhere.

Panic had set in at 56 Garden Place, as well as on the tree limb that Jake was hanging on to for dear life. Feeling the water lap at his feet, he hoped he wouldn't fall off. The water was still rising below him and slapping against the edge of the cliff. Totally exhausted from being in a state of panic and crying for so long, he rested his head against the bough of the tree. Feeling the water lap at his backside, he drifted off to a peaceful place. He couldn't force himself to stay awake one minute longer. He felt himself being lifted up and somewhere far away, in his sleepy little mind, he thought he must be drowning.

There had been no one around to see San lift him off the branch and carry him up the steep embankment and away from the water. Jake had subconsciously heard a voice that seemed far, far away.

"*You must be aware of the dangers that the water can bring, and you must always let someone know where you are, at all times,*" the voice said, "*This is only one lesson you will learn from this.*" The voice never stopped talking, and Jake had heard everything that was said, and he wished he had been able to wake up to see who was speaking to him.

"*Just because you ran out of treasures on your part of the beach, it is still safer there than where you wandered off to play. Now the tide has taken your bucket, shovel and all the seashells you found and not to mention it could have very well taken your life along with it. So, the lesson is, it may be wiser to play in safe areas than to explore the unknown and end in peril.*"

Jake heard the words that was spoken to him in his dream. He thought he must be having a conversation with God or his guardian Angel. G-Ma had said everybody has one. He felt peaceful, and he was not afraid anymore. He knew he had heard very wise words and he would never forget them or his life's lesson for as long as he lived.

While Sarah and Adam were at the police station trying to arrange for a search party or an Amber Alert for a missing child, Eden and Eve were waiting at home hoping Jake would find his way back to them. As they had waited in the Garden of Eden, they held hands and said a prayer that Jake would be found and brought back home safely. As the prayer ended, they opened their eyes and saw San coming into the Garden with Jake in his arms. They both ran to meet him, and Jake looked so limp that Eden thought he might be dead.

"San, what happened to him, where did you find him? Is he alright?"

"I was with him the entire time," San said, assuring. "Jake had decided to go to an unfamiliar part of the beach to look for treasures, and I followed him. I knew he would be in trouble, so I waited to see what he was going to do to help himself. When he'd exhausted every avenue, he climbed up a tree and cried himself to sleep. When I was certain he was asleep," he said winking at Eden, "I lifted him off the branch and brought him home. I'll take him up to his room and lay him down on his bed, but he'll need dry clothes," he said. "I'll do that while you call Adam and Sarah." Eden ran inside and called the police station to let them both know that Jake was home safe and sound.

Sarah cried tears of joy on the ride home and being relieved, Adam had tears stinging at his eyelids too knowing his son was home safe.

When they got home, Eden told Sarah that Jake was asleep in his room and she ran up to check on him. In the meanwhile, Adam was full of questions.

"What happened, where was he?"

Eden explained that he had been on the beach and wandered off to explore other areas and got caught by high tide. Someone came along and saw him asleep in a tree and carried him home.

"What? What are you telling me, who brought him home?"

Eden had known her story sounded pathetic and full of holes but what could she say, his Guardian Angel brought him home? Well yes, she guessed she could tell him that since he knew about him now.

"Mom! What are you telling me, who brought him home?" he insisted.

She walked over to her son and took both his hands in hers and asked him to please calm down, then she smiled at her son and said, "Our Guardian Angel brought him back here Adam."

He knew he didn't have to ask any more questions and when Eden saw the tension leave his face, she repeated everything to him that San had told her. They didn't know how they were going to explain Jake's homecoming to Sarah. All she knew was that someone plucked him from a tree and carried him home while he slept. They both had known there would be more questions and she would insist on answers, so they had to be prepared. As far as Adam knew the only one who had actually seen the 'Angel' was his mother. Adam knew about him, Sarah has only heard Adam's story about his Guardian Angel, but she had only half listened, and Jake had never seen or heard about San. So now what? This would not be easy to explain. Adam suddenly got a questioning look on his face, and Eden asked him what was wrong.

"What about Eve, where does she come into this, does she know anything?" He didn't need an answer to his question when he saw his mother's face, so he dropped it because he knew she would not tell him anything more than she already had.

Both of them paced around the Garden trying to come up with a sane explanation that was reasonable and believable enough for Sarah while trying to keep her promise to San. *'Where was he anyway? He could be helping out here instead of leaving it to her discretion!'* Just then Adam said he had a thought.

"How about this Mom, we tell both Sarah and Jake it was a friend of yours and someone we have not met and that way we would not be telling a lie, and your secret will be safe. I only know about him, I've never met him, and neither has anyone else, well except Eve, does that sound viable to you?"

"I suppose we might get away with it; there is only one way to find out, let's see if it'll fly. This is absolutely awful Adam, I really don't like having to tell stories, but I have no other choice in this matter."

San had sat quietly by in the twins' room and watched Sarah lovingly look down at her son as he slept peacefully. Sheer relief had been evident on her face as she smiled and softly brushed her hand across his forehead so as not to awaken him. Standing next to her mother, Eve, from time to time would sneak a glance at San. He only had only to put his finger to his lips once, and she knew what it meant. She was very careful with her glances so she wouldn't be noticed. Suddenly Sarah straightened up and stood stark still and waited as if someone were sneaking up on her. Eve noticed, but she never uttered a word, and she never glanced in San's direction, she just waited. San was making his presence known to Sarah enough to give her a complete feeling of peace. She could not explain it, but suddenly, she didn't care how Jake got home, she was just relieved and thankful that he was. All the questions she had in the back of her mind unexpectedly did not need to be answered. Her answers were right here in front of her, asleep.

Taking Eve's hand, they quietly left Jake there to finish his sleep, and they went to join Adam and Eden in the Garden. When they saw Sarah coming, they both held their breath and waited for the myriad of questions to be thrown at them, but Sarah had just walked into Adam's arms. Holding her close, he thought, *'Here it comes'* but nothing came. He looked over at his mother with questions in his eyes, and she just shrugged her shoulders as if to tell him she didn't know what was happening either. Meanwhile, Eve was tugging on Eden's sleeve to get her attention. She looked down at her and bent to hear what she had to say. Whispering softly, she said, "San's up there," and Eden knew instantly why Sarah was so calm. It was San's way of easing her mind, and it worked. Adam was facing Eden and Eve but had not really known what was going on, so he wrinkled his eyebrows in question. Eden pointed upwards toward the house and mouthed the words that would answer his question and put him at ease.

"He's up there with Jake."

Adam relaxed and squeezed Sarah even tighter.

When Jake finally awakened he had been in a total state of confusion and his mind rushed back to the beach, the water, the panic, the tree he climbed up on for safety. He also remembered that he had cried from being afraid of being swallowed up by the ocean. He thought, too, that he must have fallen asleep in the tree and he also remembered hearing a voice in his sleep. He remembered every word the voice had said, and he repeated them over and over verbatim in his mind, but he could not remember having heard the voice before. He could hear it as plain as if he were right there in the room with him. Little did he know that San was there with him and he was going to make sure that Jake remembered his life's lesson.

Looking around his bedroom, he saw no one, but wondered again, *'How had he gotten home, and how did he get off the tree? How did he get through the water and back home?'* Oh... then he remembered how much trouble he was in, and he just wanted to stay in his room and out of sight, but a voice in his head told him to go to the Garden. It was a long trip down the stairs and through the house to the garden doors, but all of a sudden, he found himself, standing in front of the doors.

'Go out to the Garden they are all there waiting for you,' the voice said, and slowly he had opened the door and stood stark still waiting for his punishment to begin.

They all seemed to notice him there at the same time and with smiles on their faces they had rushed to him with their arms open. He had tried to tell them he was sorry, but his face was buried in everybody's hugs. Adam was the first to speak.

"Son, we are so glad you are home with us, we were really worried about you, and we are sure you have learned a lesson from this solo adventure you went on. We certainly aren't going to forget that it happened, but right now we are just so happy to have you home safe and alive." Adam continued, "You have been through a traumatic experience Jake, and we all just want you to know we are here for you if you want to talk about it, ok?" Jake smiled up at him and nodded his head and was very happy to be home safe with his family.

13

Eden thought now that the twins were older and in school that she would redecorate the bedroom next to hers for Eve. It, too, was on the same side as the canal and it had been the room her parents shared while they were alive. She had rarely gone in there since they had died, but it was time to open it up and allow life in there again. It was a beautiful room in its day, but it was outdated in décor and needed to be redone. When she'd mentioned it to Eve, she was thrilled and excited about having her own room. She had told G-Ma that she wanted to help fix it up and Eden agreed she could make most of the decisions since it was going to be hers. Together they came up with ideas for draperies, a new bedroom suite and Eve had asked if she could have a trunk like hers. Eden thought it was a good idea and pleased that she had thought of it herself. She had been thinking of a cedar chest, but Eve wanted a trunk like G-Ma's. Eden had mulled it round in her mind trying to think if she would still be able to buy one since this one was ancient. Thinking that if she could not find one, then she would have one especially handmade for her. Eden could not remember a time when she didn't have her trunk, and she hoped Eve's would mean as much to her. Since she and Eve had a great deal in common, she really wanted her to have one.

They had spent the next several weeks striping wallpaper, cleaning and scrubbing the paste off the walls so they could begin to paint. When they removed the carpet, they'd discovered a beautiful oak hardwood floor in perfect condition. Taking the bed apart, Eden called Goodwill and asked if they'd come and pick up the old suite, knowing it would go to a deserving family. Standing in the big empty room, Eden knew that Eve had a lot of decisions to make since she was the one who was going to choose colors and furniture. She'd spent endless hours leafing through magazines and catalogs. When she found exactly what she'd wanted, she dog-eared each page. Of course, Eden reassured her that she had made very grown-up choices and she was very proud of her.

Choosing a white four poster bed with matching dresser and highboy, Eve also saw a matching vanity with a padded stool that could be pushed under the vanity when not in use. She showed G-Ma an oak, roll top desk that she wanted so she could use it to do homework on, and Eden said it was fine with her. She had a big room to fill, and she still had room in there for a big comfy chair if she wanted one, so she chose a rose-colored lounge chair. Calling the furniture store, Eden ordered what they had chosen, and while they waited for it to arrive, they had a few days to get the painting done, and the draperies hung. They worked at it every spare moment they had, and once they'd finished, they waited only one day for the furniture to arrive.

The furniture truck had pulled up in front of the brownstone and Eve was quite excited since all the stuff that was being delivered had been her choices. She was a very happy young lady. Some of the furniture needed to be assembled so Eden began the chore of reading diagrams and finding her collection of tools while Eve stood by ready to help and fetch in any way she could. Eden was quite adept at assembling since she had learned how to be independent a long time ago. There had never been anyone she could count on for that sort of thing. Finally, everything was ready to be placed in the room where Eve wanted them to be. With a few throw rugs here and there, it was ready for Eve to move into and she was overjoyed to be sleeping in the room next to G-Ma. Afterwards, it was time to concentrate on getting the frilly things out of Jake's room and make it into a guy's room.

The time had come for Eden to tell Jake he was getting a bedroom make-over too. He'd been as happy as his sister was to finally have a room of his own. There wasn't much that he wanted changed except to get the frilly and sissy stuff out of his room. When she mentioned that she thought he would want more than Eve's things out of there, he thought about it for a minute, he said he'd like to have a bigger bed.

"I'm not fussy G-Ma, but if there is anything you'd like to do in here to change it a bit, I don't mind."

"Are you sure Jake, I can do more than a few things in here for you?"

"Sure G-Ma, I'll like whatever you decide to do." She gave him a hug and told him he was so easy to please. She said she'd see what she could do to make his room comfortable for him.

Eden had gone ahead and ordered a huge captain's bed and an armoire with a matching desk and chair. She also ordered a big comfy brown leather chair for him. She'd decided she was going to have shelves installed on one wall to hold his prized models. She put some of his things in another room for him to use for a few nights while she went to work in his. She called Goodwill again to come over and pick up his furniture, and since there were so many unfortunate families out there, they were more than happy to get her call so soon after the last pick up. They were there in record time, and she was pleased to be able to help the needy.

109

She had already picked out paint when she was getting Eve's room ready. Once his room was empty of furniture, drapes, and pictures, she'd pulled all the nails out of the walls and filled the holes. Laying the drop clothes out around the floor, she started the task of painting. The room was huge, but with rollers, she was finished in a few hours. Taking a break, she went downstairs for a cup of tea and a sandwich and just as she sat down to eat it, San was at the other end of the table.

"Nice job, Little One." Eden blushed a bit and told herself to stop being ridiculous. "Oh really, and where were you when I needed some help?" she teased.

He was leaning back in the chair with one leg stretched out full length and Eden took notice of him sitting there so relaxed. As she followed the length of him with her eyes, thoughts of their age difference crept in again. He seemed to be an old man back then, but since she had a few more years onto herself, he was not that old looking after all. She couldn't remember when it happened, but he was not as rough looking either. He never was a 'dirty' person, but back then he had looked bedraggled to her but, for the era, maybe it was 'cool' to be dressed that way. He had not seemed to have aged hardly at all, but now that she had, they seemed to be approximately the same age. She was looking at him differently now, and she didn't know why. There was a part of her that was a little bit scared and yet excited at the same time. For some reason, she got flustered now whenever he appeared. To clear the thoughts from her mind, she asked him if he wanted to help her and he accepted. It surprised her for a second or two because he always disappeared before she was finished with him.

"You do?"

"Of course, why not?"

"Because you've never been around to help before, it seems strange that you are now, that's all."

"You've never asked for my help before, Eden," he reminded her.

When she thought about his response, all she could say was, "You're right San, I never have, so, are you ready?"

Telling her that he was, they both went up to Jake's room.

"What am I going to be doing up here?"

"You're going to help me install shelves."

"For Jake's models?"

Eden just laughed and shook her head, thinking he'd been there all along.

"You are so predictable," she said, jokingly. She had everything in the room they needed to work with, and it was going to be a lot easier with someone to help her. Once they had gotten started, the shelving was up on the wall in no time. And right on time, the furniture arrived, and Eden went downstairs to let them in. She asked them to follow her up the stairs so she could show them where to put it. They had done as she asked. Tipping them for their service, they left her an invoice and were on their way. San stood by unnoticed to everyone except to Eden, of course, and when they had left, she told him to get busy. This time the furniture had already been assembled by the delivery men and just needed to be placed.

"Where would you like to put the furniture, Eden?"

She directed him as they each carried an end. The captain's bed was placed quite nicely and centered on the largest wall. The desk and chair went in front of the huge window for plenty of light when he studied or put models together, and the armoire went on the wall where Eve's bed once was, which was the second largest wall. They put the brown leather chair in a corner by itself with a small table beside it.

The room looked totally different when they'd finished. San held the ladder for Eden while she hung the drapes up on the six-foot windows for the final touch. Finally, after one last run with the vacuum, she placed an area rug in front of his bed, and a scatter mat in front of the leather chair. San helped her put the bedding on the bed. Standing back for a final look, she was pleased with the outcome and thanked San for all his help. He told her to wait for his bill before she thanked him and they both laughed at his attempt at being humorous. Eden had one more job to do before she could actually say she was done. She had gone to the spare bedroom and brought Jake's stuff back and put it all in his room for him to put away when he got home from school. San sensed that his presence was no longer needed and when she got back he was gone.

When it was time for Jake to be home from school, Eden met him downstairs at the front door.

"Hi, G-Ma."

"Hi Jake, I have a surprise for you!"

Following her upstairs, she covered his eyes at the top of the stairs, to keep him from peeking and lead him to the doorway of his bedroom. He could not help but giggle with excitement. When she had taken her hands away, he just stood there with his mouth open for a few seconds. Slowly, Jake walked in and looked around at all the changes she had made and then he broke into a smile. She absolutely adored the look on his face as he ran over to her, wrapped his arms around her in a big squeeze and thanked her over and over.

"This is so cool G-Ma! Oh wow, look at my models! I love the furniture too G-Ma!" He was full of excitement as he tried to take it all in at once.

Eden giggled over his excitement and finally left him alone to look over everything and get used to his new things. He had minor rearranging to do now, and she knew he would want to put things in their proper places. Full of happiness, he could not wait to show his mom and dad and, of course, his sister. When everyone got home, they all gathered in his room as he showed them the finished project. After all the oohs and aahs were over, they told him what an awesome room he had, and he just beamed. Adam and Sarah thanked Eden for all her hard work and generosity, for both bedrooms and for making the twins happy. As usual, Eden shrugged it off and told them it was her pleasure and that she was happy to be able to please her grandkids.

14

Sarah had begun to get restless and decided to finally do something for herself. She had been a stay-at-home mom long enough and felt her presence was no longer needed as much now. The twins had been in school for several years, Eden was home all day, and Sarah had to admit that Eden spent more time with them than she did. She talked it over with Adam to get his opinion and approval.

"I think there are great opportunities out there for you and you should do whatever you want because the possibilities are endless."

"I feel like my time isn't being well spent here at home or with the kids and I thought that now would be a good time to be thinking about other projects."

"Are you planning to find a part-time job or start a business of your own or what do you have in mind?"

"I'm thinking about going to nursing school."

He was thrilled with her choice and looked at her with a smile. He was very pleased that she wanted to become a nurse especially when they were so badly needed.

"If that's what you want then I think you should consider doing it."

"I've already done a bit of research to find out the details, and if you think we can afford it, then I can make a decision. But in the meanwhile, I think we should talk to Mom and let her know what we've been discussing and see if she is okay with it too."

Going downstairs, they found Eden in the den reading. They asked if they could interrupt for a few minutes and she laid her book on her lap and asked them to sit down and tell her what was on their minds. Sarah told her everything that she and Adam had discussed, and Eden was visibly taken aback. Sarah thought that this was not going to work out and when she asked Eden what was wrong, it was Sarah's turn to be stunned. She assured her there was nothing wrong, but she fell silent for a few minutes. They both wanted to know if Eden was okay with Sarah not being there full time for the twins and she assured them it would not be a problem since she was always home anyway. Eden was quiet for a few more minutes trying to put her words together in her mind before speaking again. What she was thinking made her uncomfortable to ask, but she continued anyway.

"What about financing for this new career, Sarah?"

"I haven't come up with anything firm yet, but I could apply for student loans although I'm not quite sure how to go about it. I can ask for details when I go to register for classes and hopefully I can get direction from the school."

"Nonsense!"

Both Sarah and Adam were startled at the tone she'd taken, and it was certainly unexpected.

"You don't need student loans, Sarah, leave that to the people who really need the assistance, I will pay for your tuition fees."

Now it was Sarah's turn to be stunned, and she had no idea what to say to her mother-in-law. Adam admired his mom so much and loved her for her generosity. She had done so much for them already by putting him through medical school, giving them a place to live and taking such good care of the kids not to mention easing their financial burdens over the years.

"It's because of the money that I've waited so long to make a decision about my career."

"I've often wondered about that Sarah, about what you wanted to do, but felt it was not my place to ask questions and so, I waited for you to make the decision."

She reassured Sarah about the money and told her when she was ready to enroll; the money would be there. She asked her which school she had chosen, and she told her it was the Kanyon Beach Nursing College just down the street and close enough for her to walk to classes.

"And this is what you really want to do, Sarah?"

"Yes, Mom it is. I've thought about it for a long time and feel this is the right time for me."

"Well, my dear, I think you've made a wise decision, and you'll make a wonderful nurse."

"Thanks, mom," were the only words she could manage to get out of her mouth as she went across the room and put her arms around her mother-in-law.

Going upstairs to her room, Eden closed the door, went to her trunk and opened it. She pulled out an envelope and counted out what she thought she needed and put the envelope back and closed the trunk lid. Standing up, she turned to tuck the money inside her handbag and nearly ran into San. Gasping, she bumped right into his chest.

"San! Do you have to do that? Do I have to put a bell on you, so you won't scare the daylights out of me?"

San chuckled, and it was the familiar sound that Eden was used to hearing. She slipped the money into her pocket until later. San had been familiar and comforting to her since she was a little girl. He had gotten her through many situations and helped her numerous times and in a hundred different ways and here he was again.

"That was a very generous gift you just provided for Sarah, Little One, and also, I like what you've done with the twins' rooms."

Beaming up at him, she knew she had done a good job, and she thanked him again for his help with Jake's room. He loved her smile.

"I had a lot of fun doing it, and it pleased me to be able to make the children happy," she said.

"They are happy, and I especially love the leather chair in Jacob's room," he added.

She said the name 'Jacob' while cocking her head to one side. In a low voice, she repeated it to herself but loud enough so that she could hear it.

"Jacob?" she said.

As she repeated the name, San asked her what she was thinking about (as if he didn't know) She gave him a look that said as much, and he chuckled again, and so did she. This reminded her of how much fun it was having him around.

"Remember when I took care of the twins while Adam and Sarah were on their honeymoon?"

"I do."

"It was then, that I gave him the name 'Jake' and hearing you, just now, call him Jacob, I'd almost forgotten that it's his birth name."

"Indeed, it is, Eden."

"Well, I think it's time we did something about that, don't you?"

"I do, indeed. Giving him back his birth name is a great gift."

"I think so too San, Jake... er... Jacob wouldn't be here today if you hadn't rescued him off the beach that awful day, San, thank you again for being there and for bringing him home safely."

"You're welcome, Little One, I am always with them just as I am with you."

Looking at San, she felt grateful for him. Impulsively walking over to him, she put her arms around him before she even realized what she was doing. Flabbergasted, San just stood for several seconds with his arms suspended in mid-air before gently folding them around her back. When his arms touched her, she closed her eyes and enjoyed the peaceful feeling of his presence. Coming back to her senses she had opened her eyes, realizing where she was. Releasing him from her hug, he felt her let go of him, and he dropped his arms. Eden took a step back not knowing what to say or do.

"You don't call me 'Little One' very much anymore, and it felt good hearing it again," she said.

"No, I guess I haven't since Little Eve came along, and it got transferred to her."

"I didn't realize how much I missed it until you just said it. Looking at him for a long moment, he asked her what was bothering her. Walking over to him again, she asked him to just stand there. Looking at her, he stood in front of her, just as she'd asked, and she walked into his arms again. Putting her hands on his back, her fingers spread out and she laid her cheek against his chest and waited. Wrapping his arms around her again, he laid his cheek on the top of her head. Standing in the middle of her room, they held each other. Eden had been experimenting with her feeling, and she wanted to know if she would feel the same way as the first hug and it surprised her that she did. She closed her eyes for a few moments longer then stepped away... *'Now what?'* she thought.

"Yes indeed, now what," he asked, reading her thoughts.

It had surprised her for a moment when he asked, but she should have known better than to be surprised at anything when it came to him.

"It felt comfortable, and I was experimenting to see if it would feel the same as the first time."

"And?"

"Yes, it did." That was all she said, and she blushed as she admitted it to him. Stepping farther back from him, she was unsure of her feelings and didn't know quite what to say. Turning away, she slid her hand into her pocket, brought the money out and slipped it into a side pocket in her handbag and started to say something to San, but he was gone.

"You are the most infuriating man San Taman!"

Speaking into the air, she was frustrated at not knowing why she was so shaken up or even why he infuriated her. *What was going on inside her?'* she thought. Determined, she pushed thoughts of him out of her head so she could concentrate on the list of things she had to do. Taking a pad and pen from her desk drawer, she began to make her 'to do' list for the next day. She tucked the list in the side pocket with the money and went downstairs to busy herself in the kitchen not realizing how late it was. San's touch had given her an adrenalin rush and would likely take her hours to calm down. She thought she would have known better than to allow him to do that to her. Then, of course, it never crossed her mind till now that maybe he had been frustrated as well.

Going back to her room, later that evening, she prepared for bed but had a feeling that she was not alone. Taking a long leisurely bath helped relax her, and she took extra time brushing her hair. When she felt ready for bed, she had a peaceful, easy feeling as she drifted off to sleep and her last thoughts went back to the comfort of San's arms. He had watched her from a distance until she was in a sound sleep, then he had walked over to her bed and, ever so gently, touched her hair and then he was gone...

Eden had gotten up early the next morning to prepare for her day. She wanted to spend a little time with the twins before they went to school. It was decided between Eden and Sarah that whomever arrived in the kitchen first, would make breakfast. It happened that Sarah had prepared breakfast for them that morning. Eden got a cup of coffee and joined them at the table. She usually encouraged them to talk and discuss things openly and today was no exception. They told her how much they enjoyed their separate rooms and being able to close the door for privacy. The excitement was still there in their voices as they rambled on about the beautiful new rooms and how much more room they had to do their own thing.

As Eden had listened, her mind went back to her conversation with San and then turned her attention to her grandson.

"Jacob?"

"Yes G-Ma?" he said without hesitation.

"I've decided from now on I'd like to call you Jacob again, is that ok with you?"

"I'd like that G-Ma, no one at school calls me Jake."

"Really? Why?"

"When I first started school, and the teacher asked me what my name was, I told her it was Jacob, so everyone calls me Jacob now."

"I'm so happy to hear that, I thought it would be difficult for you to go back to your birth name. We've been calling you Jake since you were a baby."

"I like my real name G-Ma, no one else has a nickname only me, so I would like to be called Jacob again.

"I think that's a wonderful idea 'Mr. Jacob' and so you shall."

She was teasing him, and he knew it, but he loved it when she did. They had finished their breakfast in the usual fashion while talking about their plans for the day. Eden told them to come straight home from school, and they assured her they would.

~

Putting on her jacket, Eden left the house midmorning. Heading into the college, she asked to see the administrator. She sat and waited for several minutes and noticed a woman walking toward her. She stood to greet her, and they introduced themselves, and she followed her into her office.

"What can I do for you today?"

"I'm here to finalize the financing for my daughter-in-law who is going to begin classes here." She gave her Sarah's name and the administrator told Eden that she remembered the conversation with the young lady. She had pulled her file and told Eden what the total tuition was, and she paid the full amount. Waiting while she took the time to count it, she got a receipt. Thanking the lady, she wished her a good day and headed down the street to the bank. On her way, she saw something in a store window, and she made a mental note to stop there on her way home.

~

Eve had collected gems on a regular base and had made enough for a considerable deposit, and when Eden put the money in her account, she had also added the same amount to Jacob's. She had been doing this for so long it was a normal, regular routine for her now. At least twice a month she'd go down to the bank for her grandchildren. When she made the deposits, that day, though, she asked the teller for a printout of the two accounts. The teller did as she requested and when she passed her the pages, she just folded them in half, tucked them into her purse, thanked her and left. She remembered to make her other stop before heading home. She still had a good part of the afternoon left, so she was in no big rush to go home. She had gone into the shop to search for a gift for Sarah. Spotting a beautiful briefcase, she thought it would be perfect for Sarah to use for college and as she walked idly around the shop, she also found a matching organizer for class schedules. Asking the lady to gift wrap them, she put them both in a shopping bag for easier carrying. Paying for her purchases, she thanked her and headed home.

At the top of the steps of her house, she glanced over and saw San leaning against the lamppost smiling at her, as he'd done all those years before. Her heart pounded at the sight of him, and she turned away for only a moment to find her house key, and when she turned back to look, the spot was empty. Unlocking the door to let herself in, she took her purchases upstairs to her room. She had known there wouldn't be anyone home, so she had the house to herself for a little while.

Going into Jacob's room to collect the laundry from his hamper, she looked around at how neatly he kept his room. *'He was such a good boy,'* she thought and smiled with pride. She then went to Eve's room to collect her things, and her room was just as tidy as Jacob's with everything in its place. Standing there, she thought about the joy they had brought to her life. Going into her own room, she collected her laundry and took it all downstairs to the laundry room. Putting the laundry in, she got the machine started and heard Sarah come in.

"Mom, are you home?"

"I'm in the laundry room, Sarah."

"I was at the college today to register, and they told me everything has been taken care of, Mom, I don't know how I can ever thank you for what you are doing for me."

"Just continuing with your education is enough Sarah, no thanks needed, we're family, and that's what we do." Standing there in the middle of the laundry room, the two women hugged for a few seconds. Being fond of her, Eden felt that Sarah deserved this chance and she was happy to be of help to her.

"I have a gift for you, come and see."

Beaming, she took Sarah's hand, and they climbed the stairs together. When they got to her room, she handed her the shopping bags, and Sarah's face lit up.

"What's this?" she squealed as she pulled the big gift-wrapped present out. Tearing off the paper, she saw the beautiful, deep

124

burgundy leather briefcase she could not believe her eyes. "Mom, it's beautiful!"

"Open the other one, too," Eden said, pointing to the bag.

"The other one?"

"Yes, there's another one in the bag."

Looking inside, she pulled it out, opened it, saw the matching organizer and she had actually been speechless for a few seconds.

"Mom, these are both so lovely! Thank you so much, how did you know I would need these?"

"Mothers know everything, and there's something else I want to discuss with you, Adam and the children as soon as Adam has a spare minute."

"Actually, he's due home soon, for a change, so I'll let him know you want a few minutes."

Eden thanked her for offering to remind Adam. Sarah thanked her again for the gifts and Eden went to the kitchen to start supper while Sarah headed for the third floor.

Eden managed a few moments alone with Eve before the family gathering. Not wanting her to be surprised at what was going to be said later and reminded her again of their secret. Eve told her she understood and went with Eden to the family room.

"Hey, Mom, what's up?" Adam asked as he kissed her hello.

Focusing her attention on each one, she began to tell them why she had asked them to join her and added that it concerned them all, so no one interrupted her as she began to speak.

"Several years ago, well no, longer than that, actually," she said, "it was when you were on your honeymoon." Wagging her finger back and forth at both Adam and Sarah, indicating, she was talking about them, and they both nodded that they understood.

"I opened up savings accounts for Jacob and Eve."

"You did?" Adam asked.

"Yes, I did, Son. I wanted to start a college fund for them, and since then I have made deposits in both accounts on a regular basis. Today I went to the bank to make another deposit and asked for a printout sheet for each account." Reaching into her sweater pocket, she pulled out the sheets of paper, unfolded them and began to speak again. "I think it's time I brought this to your attention now in case; God forbid, something was to happen to me, then you'd have access to the accounts. I'll still make regular deposits as I've always done but you need to know the account numbers to make withdrawals when the time is right." Looking down at the two sheets, she gave one to Adam and one to Sarah. They both had the same amount, and as they each turned the page around to look at it they both gasped at the same time.

"Mom, My God! How did you do this?"

"Never mind how I did it, Adam, it's done. It's for the children's education which is already paid."

"Mother, there's fifty thousand dollars in each of these accounts!"

"Yes son, I'm aware of the balances. I have both bank books in the den in the safe. The money will be used when they begin university, and in the meanwhile, the money will be drawing interest over the next several years. There will be enough in there to cover the cost of their education. If they choose to leave here and go out of town to other universities, there will be enough to cover living expenses as well. I know the children are still young, but it is never too early to start preparing for their future."

"Well, Mom, once again you managed to leave us speechless, surprised and totally grateful for what you've done."

"I didn't call you all here for a round of thanks, I wanted you and Sarah to be aware of Jacob and Eve's accounts and how they are to be used."

"Thank you, Mom, so very much, you have taken care of us all, first by paying my way through medical school, you're paying Sarah's way through nursing school, and now you've seen to it that the twins are taken care of as well. May I ask how you are doing all this?"

"Good investments, Adam."

That was all she said as she winked at Eve who was sitting by taking it all in and admiring her grandmother. She could not love her more than she did at this moment. Jacob did not have a lot to say, but as he observed his grandmother in action, it made him realize just how very much his G-Ma loved her family.

15

Jacob had often thought of the special connection his grandmother had with his sister, he didn't know what it was, and he was not jealous of it, but there was something that bonded them, and it had made him curious. He'd always known that Eve had an imaginary friend. He'd known it for several years because he used to hear her talking to him or her, he was never sure which. Sometimes his curiosity got the better of him, and he would take a few minutes to eavesdrop, whenever he could do it unnoticed. Most of the conversations had to do with the broken glass she'd picked up off the beach and brought home. He could never figure out what all the fuss was with that junky old glass! Then, he had got to wondering where it had all disappeared. He saw it when she brought it home then after her conversation with her friend, it was gone. *'Had she thrown it out after realizing it was junk?'* he wondered. She'd spend every free minute she had on the beach collecting that stuff, then she'd bring it home, described each piece to her 'friend,' and then the pieces disappeared! *'Where did they go and who in their right mind would want them?'* he thought. Somebody had wanted them, they had gone somewhere! He was full of curiosity but did not want to ask too many questions. *'If these pieces of glass that she called her treasures, were that important to her, would you not think they would be in a collection bowl or glass bottle or a case for safekeeping. There was nothing here! Where were they?'* He somehow thought he wouldn't get a straight answer even if he did ask.

All those one-sided conversations she'd had were pretty boring at times, but they would keep her occupied for hours. He guessed if he could not figure out who his sister was talking to then he would never figure out who G-Ma talked to either! Maybe that was what they had in common. *'Did they each have an imaginary friend or was it the same one?'* He never did get up enough courage to ask them because then he would have to admit he had been eavesdropping on them and he didn't think that would sit well with anyone, so he kept his curiosities to himself. Besides, he thought, G-Ma had been chatting with someone since he could remember so maybe Eve was trying to imitate her and made up her own 'friend.'

Then suddenly Jacob had thought he might like to have a special someone like them, to talk to and be friends. San was sitting in Jacob's brown leather chair watching him feel sorry for himself. He wanted to put his arms around him and tell him he was never alone. Jacob felt the slightest hint of a breeze in his room for just a few seconds, and he looked around to see if anyone was there. Although he had not seen anyone it felt like there was someone else in his room. He flopped down on his leather chair and wondered why it felt so warm. San wished Jacob could feel his arms around him, but he knew he couldn't. Jacob experienced a very comforting feeling of something familiar, but he didn't know or understand why.

San spent a lot of time in Jacob's room with him. He pretty much shared his time with all of them almost equally, but Eden would always take priority. The warm thoughts about her in his arms came flooding back to him as he had sat in Jacob's leather chair. Leaning his head back against the chair, he closed his eyes for a few moments to allow the feelings to flow over him in waves. Something was happening to him that he had never experienced before, and it had taken him completely by surprise.

San had been around for a very long time, and this was the first 'real' family he'd had. It was the first opportunity he had to be a part of a family and be so close to them. He'd watched Eden grow from a charming little girl to an adorable teenager, then to a loving, independent single mother and now, a gracious and beautiful older woman. He adored her, he always had, and try as he might he could not remember a time when he did not love her. Watching her grow into this magnificent person absolutely overwhelmed him. He was more than aware of what a great mother she had been and now as a devoted grandmother. Taking these two beautiful children, claiming them as her own and loving them, as if they were her own flesh and blood, takes a special person, but then again, she had always been special to him.

He did not know how to handle this most recent turn of events. He could still feel Eden in his arms, and he didn't know quite what to do with these new-found feelings. He raised his head from the back of the chair and opened his eyes as Jacob brought him from his thoughts. He didn't know if he was grateful or sad for the distraction. Jacob, feeling the warmth in his chair, turned to the side to cuddle but did not realize he was cuddling in San's lap and he welled up with feelings of familiarity. San had rocked him many, many times and held him exactly that way. It had caused San to hold him as close as he could and then he planted a kiss on the top of his head... Jacob nodded off in San's arms.

16

Adam had worked long hours to get where he was. The inside of the hospital had become as familiar to him as his own home. He was grateful to have such a loving and supportive family. He never got grief from anyone when he had to spend days on end at the hospital. Napping for a few minutes or hours, here and there whenever he could, before another call came in. It had been well worth it, and he had finally gotten the title he had worked for so hard. He was now a Doctor, and although his dream was finally realized, the real work had just begun. It had been a difficult decision for him trying to make up his mind in which field he wanted to specialize. He loved every aspect of the medical profession. He worked in every department that he was allowed. There was not one area of it that he did not love. His first few years in residency were spent doing everything possible to learn whatever was necessary for future use. Being there every spare minute, he'd never considered it a hardship. He was fully aware that most doctors usually decided on their specialty before med school. Being different, he wanted to try it all instead of concentrating on just one thing, but it was time for a decision.

He'd tried it all and, in the end, he felt that working in the ER and Out-Patients Department were the most fulfilling for him. He wanted to get the benefit of working in these two places, and he decided to open up his practice in the hospital's Medical Centre. Taking afternoon appointments, he began to build his practice while working mornings in ER and Out-Patients. It was only an elevator ride down if he was needed for emergencies.

Once he had his plan put together, he had gone up to the third floor to see what was available for office space. What he'd had found, took him completely by surprise. There was a lovely corner office available, and he could not believe it had not been snatched up. The office had been professionally cleaned when the last occupant had moved out, and it was stipulated in his contract that he would be bound to the same clause. It was well laid out and consisted of everything he needed. There was a reception area, his office for receiving patients and an examination area. It came completely furnished which had eliminated time and the expense of buying new furniture and shopping around to find new stuff. He was excited to finally start his private practice. This would not be as easy as working in the hospital and carrying a stethoscope around your neck and writing notes in charts. This is going to be his office and his patients and his responsibility. They were people he had met here in the hospital, and they chose him as their family physician way before he was ready for his practice. He had worked with them in emergency situations, and they came to love and respect him as a doctor.

Looking for a medical receptionist, he placed an ad in all the appropriate places and hoped whoever answered it would be competent. With a list of possible applicants to interview, he prepared a list of questions and had them ready to use.

Some of the questions were not medically related, but he had thrown them in anyway hoping at least a couple would suit him for callbacks. The interviews were set up and were to take place in his office. There were a few eliminations soon into the question period, and Adam had begun to lose hope of finding someone on his first attempt. He thought he would have to place a newer ad and try again. This was more difficult than he had originally thought it would be. The ad specifically stated, 'medical receptionist,' and most of the applicants had little or no experience in medical terminology whatsoever. *'This was not a difficult concept,'* he thought, *'either you are, or you are not qualified and if you are not, then why apply in the first place?'* These people had wasted his time and basically, their own as well. As soon as more resumes began arriving, Adam read every one, page for page. It was hard to believe that the people who applied, had even bothered.

This had gotten redundant, and Adam was slowly losing faith. He had thought about placing the ad in places where these types of people would not have access to them, like the hospital bulletin board.

Preparing himself for more disappointments, he waited for the last applicant to arrive. Clearly, he was losing interest with the interviews and was going over in his head how to word the next ad specifically. Looking up briefly, he nodded to the next applicant as to where to sit, while mentally preparing himself for this last interview of the day. Lifting his head to introduce himself to her, he began to ask her the same round of questions he'd already asked a dozen other girls only with less interest this time. Noticing his lack of enthusiasm, she answered his first question. Then she asked him if he had had a rough day and it took him totally by surprise.

"Why do you ask?"

"It's late in the day, and I suspect you've been doing interviews all afternoon, and by the look on your face, I'd say without much success."

He thought it was very perceptive of her and he leaned back in his chair in total fatigue.

"This has been worse than a day in the ER," he admitted.

"I'm sure it was."

She began by answering his first question in detail, and as the interview moved along, he noticed it was taking shape quite nicely. Taking an interest, he asked her several more questions and realized this was the only applicant who actually knew her stuff. He flipped back several pages to recall her name. Finding it, he looked up at her. "Your name is Rachel?"

"Yes, it is," she said, answering his question while Adam was trying very hard to stifle a smile.

"Is there something wrong, Doctor?" she asked.

"No, Rachel, there isn't, it's just that I have a house full of biblical names and here you are with one, and it seems you are the only one who is qualified for this position. Is that weird or is it just me?" he asked. He couldn't help but laugh after that last statement, and if Rachel had known his story, she would have thought it was funny too. She was just happy to know he was not laughing at her.

Composing himself, he looked at her and realized he had put her in a very uncomfortable situation. Apologizing to her, he offered her the job which she had readily accepted. Telling her the start date and the salary he was offering, she left when they were both in complete agreement.

Filling the receptionists' position, he began writing up an ad for a part-time office nurse. Surely there would be someone who needed part-time work with flexible hours and would be available for a few hours in the afternoons for his appointments. Staffing a nurse was a safety feature he wanted for his office. With all the malpractice suits going on these days, he could not avoid being careful. He did not want to be put into a compromising situation where it was his word against theirs. He had heard of these situations arising while he was still in training. Often, the hospital chose to settle out of court to avoid the publicity of a lawsuit and be discredited in the medical profession. Mostly, the charges were bogus, and a payout was easier than trying to prove their innocence, which in most cases was impossible. So, Adam wanted a jump start on that issue from day one. Finishing his ad, he took it to the main floor and tacked it up on the board.

~

Sarah was getting her feet wet in nursing school. She knew already that she loved nursing, she just had not realized just how much. When the first several months of classroom studies were behind them, they were each given a list of possible places to go and look for an on-the-job-training position. They were told the positions would be free of charge to the employer since it was training experience. On the list were several hospitals, medical centers, clinics, nursing homes, private practices and any medical facility that would be beneficial to their training. It was up to them to convince someone to hire them as well as their choice as to where they wanted to work. They would still have morning classes, but their afternoons were free to do hands on training.

One of the places on Sarah's list was the Kanyon Beach Memorial Hospital where Adam worked. On her first free afternoon, she went job hunting. It was an easy walking distance for her, so she decided to go there first to see what was available. Arriving at the hospital, she had asked to see someone in personnel and waited until someone appeared to speak to her. Finally called into an office, she introduced herself and told the lady why she was there. The personnel officer told her they had a bulletin board located near the staff room and maybe she should begin there. Telling her where it was located, Sarah thanked her for her time and went in search of the board. After asking a few people for more directions, she found it. There had been several ads tacked on the board, and she read every one. One, in particular, caught her eye, and she thought it might be just what she was looking for since it stated, 'flexible hours.' The ad read, 'Wanted: part-time nurse with flexible schedule to assist in doctor's office, apply on third floor in medical centre,' It gave the office number and directions to get there, and she thought, '*Why not, I might get lucky today.*' Writing the information down in her organizer, she headed for the elevator. Getting in, she pressed three and waited for her ride to stop.

The doors opened, and Sarah stepped out. Looking around to orient herself, she opened her organizer to read the directions again. She was thinking about how handy her organizer was and how many times she had used it since she started nursing school. She smiled and thought of Eden when a familiar voice broke her thoughts...

"You look lost..."

Turning, she broke into a happy smile.

"Adam! Hi!" she said, surprised and glad to see him, as well as a familiar face.

"Who are you looking for?" he asked.

"I don't know yet, she admitted." She told him about the on-the-job-training program at school, and she came in search of a job.

"That's a great idea!" he said.

"Yes, it is, and the best part is,' she said, 'whoever hires me gets free service since we are in training. Maybe you can steer me in the right direction."

She opened her organizer and showed him the ad she had copied down.

Smiling at her, he waved his arm. "Follow me," he said.

"Oh, thank you, Adam, I am not the least bit familiar with this area of the hospital, and I appreciate your help."

Leading her into his office, she still didn't know where she was. She'd been too busy with school that she hadn't had time to see his office or help him in any way to get ready for his opening. But she figured it must be nearby since she ran into him just outside.

"Please, sit down Nurse Sarah."

"Adam?"

"You are here for an interview, aren't you?"

"Yes, I am."

"Ok then, shall we begin?"

She was totally shocked. "This is your office... and your ad?"

"Indeed, it is, now shall we get to the reason why you're here?"

They both laughed and said at the same time, "What are the odds?"

~

Adam's practice was up and running and doing very well. It hadn't taken long for word to spread that his practice was open and ready on the third floor. Being at hospital for years, he was well known to those he'd treated in the ER or outpatients. Once he'd established his practice, many wanted to be taken on as his patients. Not long after his opening, he was fully booked every afternoon.

17

One morning Adam was in the ER for his shift, and as usual, it was chaotic. He had been there since early morning, and it had not slowed down, not even a little bit. It was one case right after another and backed up to overload. He noticed one man who had been in the waiting area for a long time. He didn't know if he had been overlooked if he had forgotten to register himself when he came in or if his problem was not serious enough to rate a doctor, but he seemed to have been there longer than anyone. He brought it to a nurse's attention and asked her why he was still there. She explained that she didn't think he had registered at the front desk. Adding that he was not a regular, she said she had not seen him before.

Adam was thinking just the opposite, he did seem familiar. *'Did he know him from somewhere?'* he thought. He asked her to go over and ask him if he needed attention, write a chart up on him and show him to a cubicle and that he'd be with him as soon as he finished with his next patient. He glanced over at him again, and at the same time the stranger looked up and they stared at each other for a few seconds. Shaken to his roots, Adam nodded his head and turned away to tend to his other waiting patient. He was having difficulty concentrating on the case at hand, and he could not understand why. He had gone from case to case in a heartbeat with total focus and control so why could he not get this man out of his mind long enough to treat the person who needed him right now? Finally shaking off the strange feelings, he concentrated on his patient. Writing up the information on the chart, he gave further instructions for a follow-up appointment at his office. Giving him the number, he asked him to call his receptionist about an afternoon appointment. Closing the chart, he returned to the waiting area.

Passing him a new chart, the nurse told him the patient, he'd asked about, was in cubicle four. He was about to pull the curtain open, to the cubicle, when he flipped the cover on the chart. Glancing down at the top of the page to find a name, he stopped dead in his tracks. His mind was going in several different directions, yet he wasn't really focusing on any one thing. Feeling his heart racing, his mouth was suddenly as dry as a cork. He wanted so badly to turn around and find another doctor to call upon, but he was already halfway through the curtain that was still draped on his shoulder. He thought he must look rather ridiculous standing there draped in a hospital curtain.

"Are you okay, Doc?"

"Yes, I guess I am," Adam answered, but unsure if he was telling the truth. This cannot be, he thought, reading the chart again, but the only way to be certain was to play it out.

"What can I do for you today, sir? What seems to be your problem?"

"Confusion, for one thing, loss of memory and time, is another. I'm having flashes of memory, but I'm not sure if it is in fact memory recall or not. "Do I know you, Doc?" he asked.

"Have you been here long?" Adam asked avoiding his question.

"A few days is all."

"And what brought you here?"

"It seems I bought a house here years ago and the lawyer that I had at the time had a search done on me to see if I was still alive. I guess a decision had to be made on my house and property. The taxes hadn't been paid recently, and before it went up on a tax sale, they wanted to try and find me first. I didn't know I even owned a house, here or anywhere. Why do you look familiar?" he added.

Adam looked at the man then looked at his chart again while he scribbled notes on it and when he looked up at him again their eyes met, and it was as if Adam was looking at himself in the future.

"I'm not sure, could you try and fill in a few more blanks, like perhaps, where have you been? How long have you been there? Better yet, how did you get there?" Adam stressed the word 'how' more out of curiosity than anything. The man looked off into space for a few minutes with a furrowed brow, before he spoke as if trying to think about what he'd been asked.

"It seems so much like a dream," he said. "I have snippets of memory if indeed it is a memory. Maybe it's a dream of being here, and if I was here, I don't think it was for very long. I'm sorry, I know I'm rambling, but nothing is clear to me, and I find it difficult to answer these questions if I don't know the answers to them." He ran his hand over his entire face in one swipe as if to clear his head before speaking again. He was desperately trying to recall some useful information but what he did remember did not even sound like the truth because none of it was clear, and what he thought he was remembering was all so fuzzy. "You know Doc, I'm going to tell it like I see it, okay? It's as if I have been in a hypnotic state for the past twenty some, almost thirty years."

'*Oh Boy,*' Adam said to himself, as thoughts of 'his Angel' crept in. "Please go on and tell me whatever you can." Adam wanted him to keep talking while he continued taking notes. He tried not to look at the man's face or look as if he was interested on a personal level.

"I think I've answered your questions Doc, to the best of my knowledge. And, another thing is, I don't think I left on my own. I don't remember leaving on my terms, and the weird thing about it is, it seemed like I was more carried away than going on my own. Yet, when I got there, all of my belongings, my car and everything else that I'd owned were there too. And I could hear someone talking to me the entire time, and it was not a good conversation that much I have always remembered. It was like I was programmed never to forget. 'Don't come back to the Garden,' the voice said to me over and over again. I don't know which garden he was talking about. Why would I be in a Garden? Why would I want to be in a Garden, is more the question? The voice behind it sounded quite angry and determined to get rid of me in a threatening sort of way. I have tried for years to forget the sound of his voice, but I can't."

Adam's next question needed to be asked, but he really did not want to hear the answer. He was certain he already knew what it was, as surely as he was breathing.

"Where is the house that you returned to recently?"

"It isn't very far from here actually, which is why I chose to come here. It's the closest hospital in the area."

142

Adam stared at the name on the chart for a few more seconds to clear his thoughts and try as he might his could not moisten the inside of his mouth even a little bit before he had to speak again.

"I need the house address for the chart information."

"It's 54 Garden Place," he said looking at Adam with a questioned look.

"Do you think that's the 'Garden' I keep hearing about in my mind?"

Adam ran his hand over his entire face, just as the patient had done only a few minutes before and he stopped, looked at his hand and was thinking about the same garden. Trying to avoid the same pattern he ran his hand through his hair this time, trying to compose himself.

"Why are you looking so pale all of a sudden, Doc?"

Adam felt as if he were going to faint and he sat down on a stool next to his workstation, trying to make sense of everything he had just heard. *'Could this man possibly be my father?'* His thoughts were running wild inside him as he looked down at the chart again and fixing his eyes on the name 'Luke.' "Roman, is your last name?"

"It could be Doc, it's the one I've been using all these years, but like everything else, even that is foggy to me."

When Adam regained his composure, as much as he could, he turned to his patient and asked if he could make another appointment for him at his office for the next afternoon. Luke agreed to see him, and he took out the appointment book that

Rachel kept updated for him and penciled him in for the last appointment for the next day. He told him that his office was on the third floor and gave him brief directions on how to get there once off the elevator.

18

Adam left the cubicle and went to the reception desk to leave the chart. Calling his office, he asked Rachel when his first appointment was, to be certain that nothing had changed with his schedule. She confirmed his first one was not until two thirty. Before hanging up, he told her about the appointment he had penciled in, for Luke, for the end of the next day's agenda and asked her to make the change in her records as well. He informed her that he was heading home, but he'd be back for his first appointment.

Going home, Adam tried, with everything inside him, not to look at the house next door on his way up the steps to let himself in. "Mom, are you here?"

Eden ran down the stairs with the look of horror on her face. "Adam? What's wrong? Why are you home in the middle of the day? Did something happen to one of the twins or Sarah?"

"No Mom, everyone is fine, but I really need to talk to you. Please, come into the den with me, it's important."

"Adam, you're starting to freak me out here, what is it, Son? Why are you so worked up?"

Adam was pacing back and forth across the den floor, and Eden's voice blasted him out of his jumbled thoughts.

"Adam!?"

He stopped pacing long enough to begin talking, but as soon as he opened his mouth, he began to ramble and not make sense. Eden walked over to him and put her hands on each of his arms.

"Adam, please, calm down and talk to me."

Taking a deep breath, he pulled her in for a hug and held her tightly for a few seconds, trying to gain some composure, before releasing her.

Stepping back, he slid his hands down her arms and said, "Mom, let's sit down."

He began to tell her the story of the patient he had seen less than an hour ago. "Mom, he told me he has no memory of leaving here almost thirty years ago. He felt as if he had been carried, transported if you will, out of town to another place and was told never to return to the Garden. He said he felt as if he has been hypnotized into forgetting his past. The only reason why he came back is because a lawyer tracked him down before his house was sold for taxes." Eden looked at him as if he was speaking another language and by now she was on her feet.

"Adam! What are you talking about? Why are you so worked up and agitated?"

"Mom, this guy looks exactly like me, only older!"

Instantly, the blood drained from Eden's face causing her to nearly passed out. Stumbling backwards, she reached for something to hang on to. Adam ran to grab her before she fell and sat her down on the sofa. She was totally unprepared for this.

"Mom put your head down between your knees." Holding the back of her neck, he asked, "Are you ok, Mom?" He had never seen his mother this affected by anything as she was by this.

Raising her head slowly, she looked at Adam. "What are you saying?" As the words tumbled out of her mouth, she started to cry. Adam could not remember ever seeing his mother cry. He lowered his voice and began again.

"What I'm saying Mom, is that I think this guy is my father!"

"Oh, dear God!" she said, speaking under her breath, but Adam heard it.

"He said his house is right here, next door," he said, pointing in the direction of the neighboring property, "and he said his name is Luke."

When the word 'Luke' left his lips, it was as if an angry blast of wind tore through the room! Adam nearly lost his breath as a surge of fear ripped through his entire body. It was something like he'd never experienced before.

Eden looked up just as San waved his arm in torment and wailed, "Noooooo!" in a voice that only Eden heard, and Adam felt. San cried out in a fit of fury causing the whirl in the room. San was furious, and Eden heard panic in his voice. The room was in total chaos. The power from San's fury sent papers flying in all directions and knocked over ornaments that sent glass flying all over the room. Adam's legs, weakened by fear, had caused him to fall backwards into his chair. Looking shaken and stunned, he thought a tornado suddenly struck them. Gathering his wits, he asked Eden what had just happened.

"I'm sure you know who it is, Adam."

"Yes, I suppose I do."

Eden knew it was time, and she had to tell him not only why it was happening, but the 'reason' it was happening too. "Adam," she began, "I thought I would never have to tell you this but, it seems now that I must." Sitting among the strewn papers and broken glass, he was not certain if he wanted to hear it or not.

"Are you ok Adam?" she asked. He nodded, and she went on. "I'm going to give you the condensed version right now, but later on, if you need for me to elaborate, I promise I will." Taking a deep breath, she leaned forward and began to tell Adam her story.

"Luke moved in next door, shortly after my parents were killed and about a year before you were born. Actually, he had only been next door for a few months when I met him one afternoon while I was out in my Garden." The word 'Garden' made him stiffen as he heard, 'don't come back to the Garden,' rush back to his mind. As she continued he forced himself to listen.

"He introduced himself from his side of the fence, and we chatted for a few minutes then he asked me if I would like to go out for dinner. Being alone as much as I was and as naïve as I was, I accepted, if for nothing else, then for the company. We'd had a nice dinner, we drank some wine, and as you know, I am not much of a drinker so before I knew it I was a little more than tipsy. I asked him to bring me home, and instead of leaving me at the door, he came inside. I didn't remember much after that until I woke up the next morning, sick as a dog and very confused. Reality hit me in the face when I got up off the bathroom floor and went back to the bedroom. He had raped me, Adam, while I was passed out from drinking, drunk if you will. I called the police and went through the entire police scene, the rape kit, answered all their questions as best I could, and that was the end of it. I have never heard anything about Luke until today. Well no, that isn't true either." Adam frowned questioningly, and she continued. "After the police left I went into the bathroom to take a hot bath. After I'd finished, I made up my bed with fresh sheets, climbed in and fell asleep."

San was still in the room with her and Adam, and she glanced up at him for approval, and he nodded for her to continue.

"When I woke up, I was not alone."

"What?" Adam barked impatiently, "Luke hadn't come back, had he?"

"No Son, he had not come back, it was San."

"San? Who's San?" This was the first time hearing the name.

Waving her hand around the room at the mess, she repeated his name. "San is the one who has been with me since I was a very young girl. He was there in my room, that night when I woke up. I was startled at first until I realized it was him and then I became calm. He told me I would never have to worry about Luke again, that he would take care of everything. I never felt the need to ask questions, I believed it was true. I never wanted to see Luke again, for obvious reasons, and that was the last time I ever heard his name spoken out loud. Several weeks later I was on the beach early one morning when suddenly, I'd became too weak to make it back home. I'd been alone and a little panicked and didn't know how I was going to make it back up the beach. I'd told myself that I'd rest until I felt like I would be strong enough to walk. As soon as I closed my eyes, I suddenly felt as if I was being carried, transported." Waving her hand as if describing the word 'transported.' Adam was thinking the same thing and knew the story was lining up.

"I heard a voice, as I was being carried back here, telling me he would take care of you and me. I didn't know there was a 'you' at that time. I'd made an appointment with my doctor the very next day, and she'd confirmed that I was pregnant. San knew your name even before I did." She stopped to take a deep breath before she continued. "You are well aware, by now, that you are the image of Luke and I saw that the moment I laid eyes on you, but I never let that come between me and my love for you. San has always been here with us Adam, and actually, he is the one who carried Jacob home from the beach that day when we thought he was lost. It seems there's never been a time when he has not been right here with us," she said adamantly.

Sitting quietly by, San felt it was time...

While Eden sat on the sofa, Adam sat in a chair, across from her. Walking over to the sofa, San sat down next to Eden and opened himself up to Adam.

Leaning forward, elbows on his knees and his fingertips pressed together, Adam's head was bowed as he listened to his mother's words. As San sat down beside to her, Eden stopped speaking and waited for his next move. Raising his head to speak to her, Adam saw San sitting next to his mother. Frightened at the sudden appearance of a stranger, Adam leapt to his feet. But as soon as he stood up, a calmness came over him, and he sat back down on the edge of his chair. He was speechless, to say the least, but very calm.

"Hello, Adam."

Hearing San's voice for the first time, a rather delightful feeling ran through him as if he'd just found the one thing he'd been searching for, for his entire life.

"San? You're... San?" he asked in a voice that was barely audible.

"Yes, Adam, I am... San."

Adam stood up and knowing what was coming next, San got up too. Walking to the sofa, Adam stood in front of his 'Angel' who'd been around him since before his birth. Reaching out for a handshake, San put both hands on Adam's shoulders and pulled him to his chest in a warm, wonderful hug. Overcome with emotions, Adam began to weep because of the familiar soothing touch of San's embrace. Inhaling deeply, he recognized a scent that he had smelled forever. San stood holding Adam in his arms while he sobbed and waited until Adam was ready to let go. The only words that San spoke were, "It's ok, Son."

Tears streamed down Eden's face as she watched the only two men in her life, standing in her living room, in an embrace. This was a moment she'd hoped for but thought it would never happen.

Adam finally pulled away to look at San. He couldn't think of a single word to say, but he was grinning from ear to ear like he had just met a superstar.

"San," he whispered, "I don't quite know what to say, except, thank you I guess, for my life, for which I wouldn't have if you hadn't gotten my mother off the beach that day, and for my son's life, another rescue from the beach."

San just waved his hand. "There's absolutely no need to thank me, Son."

"Daddy?" Eve said softly. She had been standing in the archway looking in on the tail-end of what had just taken place. "Are you... ok, Daddy?" Eve asked as she stood stark still. Not wanting to give their secret away, she tried not to look at San Taman or give the impression that she knew he was in the room. Looking from her daddy to her grandmother and skimming past San, she waited for someone to speak. They were startled at her appearance, and no one knew precisely what to say.

Eden looked on since Adam still was not certain if Eve actually was aware of San because his mother never confirmed either way. He could only imagine what her thoughts were, watching him standing in the middle of the room talking to... who?

"Hello, Little One," San said breaking the silence. Eve still did not move for fear of giving their secret away.

"Adam?" San said turning back to him.

"Yes?" he whispered out of the side of his mouth, so Eve wouldn't hear.

Eden could not contain her herself any longer, and she burst into laughter. "You should see the look on your face Adam," she said teasing him, as tears rolled down her cheeks. "Priceless is all I can say, I could have bought you for a nickel right then. Adam, Honey, Eve knows about San. She has for quite a while now, and she has been an angel keeping our secret all this time. We promised San that we would, and we had to honor our promise to him."

"Hi, San!" Eve said smiling at him, and Adam could see the love in his daughter's eyes for San, it was the same love he saw in her eyes when she looked at him, so he knew she regarded him as family.

This was a day that Eden, her son, and her granddaughter would not soon forget. Adam not only came face to face with his father, but he also learned what he had done to his mother and how he was conceived. He finally met the Guardian Angel that had been with him since his conception, and he remembered his mother's words again, 'He knew about you before I did.' It was no wonder he never had, in his life, felt alone and here was the man responsible for that.

He finally understood that San had run Luke out of town to protect his mother. He did not quite understand how he 'transported' things or people around from place to place and he was not curious enough to ask, and he didn't feel it was any of his business or anything that he'd understand. He knew deep in his soul that he had always loved someone he never saw, until today. He felt nothing for Luke and even less than nothing now that he knew what he'd done to his mother. How was he ever going to face this poor excuse of a man in his office the next afternoon?

153

Feeling Adam's turmoil, San walked over to him and spoke, "I think I should take care of that for you, Son."

Looking into his eyes, Adam smiled and said, "I'd really appreciate it if you could."

San nodded and placed a hand on his shoulder. "Consider it done."

Walking over to his mother, Adam hugged her. He'd had no idea of the burden she had been carrying around all those years, and he knew it must not have been easy. "I'm so sorry this happened to you Mom," he whispered.

"It's done Adam, and it was a long time ago, I've moved on Son, and now so should you. If there are any questions that you need answers to, please don't hesitate to ask."

Turning away from his mother, he picked Eve up in his arms and swung her around while giving her a big squeeze. As soon as he spun Eve around, he noticed as quickly as that... San was gone.

Eden noticed the look on his face and went over and patted him on his arm. "Get used to it Adam." And the three of them smiled at each other.

Adam looked at his watch and realized that it was nearly time for his first afternoon appointment and he told Eden and Eve he had to go back to the office.

"Say hi to mommy!"

"I will, Sweetheart, and in the meantime, I think it would be a good idea if you helped G-Ma clean up this mess," he said waving his arm around at the mess San had made.

"I will Daddy," she said, "I'll help G-Ma."

"Good girl," he said hugging them both again and headed back to the hospital.

Eden and Eve were nearly finished cleaning up the mess in the den when Jacob arrived home from school. He'd stayed later than Eve because he had soccer practice. Eden was glad he was not here for the showdown earlier. There would be no explaining that one away. As it was, she and Eve were both tagged as having loose screws. She saw the weird looks she got after a conversation with San.

Suddenly, Eden felt relieved that she had separated the twins to give them each their own space. Eve certainly felt more comfortable when San suddenly appeared in her room, and it allowed her to enjoy her time with San freely. She also needed her privacy for the transactions with him for her treasures. Spending time with San gave her the incentive she needed to search for treasures. Whenever she'd find some, she knew he would come around for a visit. It didn't matter if she found several or only one, San made each visit feel special. She never knew any other grandparent except for G-Ma, so she considered San as her special G-Pa. Sometimes she wished that Jacob had this, too, but she knew that would depend on San when he was ready. He was the only one who could make it possible for Jacob to know him and for him to have a special G-Pa as well. She was especially glad that her daddy knew about San now. She hoped that maybe someday Mommy and Jacob would know him too.

19

Adam was walking lighter, his heart felt freer. Adam's attitude had changed towards just about everything, from a few hours earlier when he left the hospital to confront his mother about Luke. He had a purpose, he felt like he belonged, and he knew his family would be better because of San. Arriving at the hospital, he headed for the elevator when he saw Sarah waiting for the doors to open. Seeing him coming, she stepped inside and held the door for him.

"Hi Honey," he said.

"Hi yourself,"

They tried to be professional at their place of work, and for the most part, they were. But today, Adam had gladness in his heart, and he was happy with the turn of events. Once the elevator doors closed, he pulled her into his arms and kissed her.

"Adam! What are you doing? We are at work!"

"Not yet we aren't!" He was teasing her and giving her another hug. She gave him a shy sideways glance before the doors opened and tried to compose herself. When Adam and Sarah walked into the office, Adam put on his Doctor's face and walked over to the reception desk.

"That appointment I penciled in for tomorrow afternoon? Please cancel it."

"It's been cancelled already, Dr. Thomas."

He nodded approvingly and went into his office. Having no desire to ask questions, he accepted what she said. He heard San's words again, 'I think I should take care of that for you, Son' and as he remembered those words his face softened into a smile...

~

Adam had just finished with his last patient for the afternoon and was busy taking last-minute notes when San appeared. When he noticed him standing by the door, he nearly jumped out of his skin. Slapping his hand against his heart, he leaped to his feet. "Oh geez!"

Realizing who it was, he smiled broadly. Although he was surprised and happy to see him, he couldn't help but ask. "How did my mother do this for so many years?"

"She got used to it and you will, too. I just popped in, quite literally, to let you know the problem has been taken care of, is there anything you need to know?"

"I don't think there is and the less I know on that topic, the better off I'll be."

"Good answer, Son."

Adam's office door was wide open since he was not with a patient. Rachel had gone home for the day, and Sarah was finishing up paperwork. She was getting things organized for the next day's shift and then she would be ready to go home as well. She didn't usually make a habit of interrupting Adam on her way out of the office. She always waited until they got home, and she knew he'd be home an hour after she arrived. As she was passing his office, she could hear his voice. It was only his voice that she heard, and she could hear a conversation with bits of laughter along with pleasant chatter and thought someone must have come in to talk to him. On her way by, she looked in and saw that he was talking to someone, but who? And where were they? She saw no one else in the room with him. He was still seated at his desk as Sarah walked up to his door.

"Adam? I thought you were finished for the day and that you were alone in here, who are you talking to?

"I'm not alone, Sarah," he said. He started to say, 'San is here' when he heard a loud 'ahem!' and he realized that Sarah could not see or hear San. Just as he said 'ahem' San tapped the door with his fingers, and it closed in her face. Jumping back, she looked at the door in disbelief. *'How did that happen? How did the door close?'* she wondered. *'Adam was at the far end of the room and unable to reach it from his desk, and he would never be that rude to her even if he was with a patient, yet the door closed on its own!'*

On the other side of the door, Adam was in stitches thinking about the look that must be on Sarah's face, and then he sobered instantly and slapped himself on the forehead with his palm.

"This is not funny, how am I going to get out of this one? And how can I explain this when I barely understand it myself!" He looked over to where San was to get a suggestion, and he was gone! "Great! Get me in trouble and then leave, nice going San!" he said shaking his head and grinning. He figured San would be a hoot if he'd stick around long enough for him to find out.

San was having fun with Adam, he had not gone anywhere, and he was still watching Adam to see how he was going to handle this with Sarah.

Knowing he had to face her sooner or later, he walked over to the door, put his hand on the doorknob, looked up at the ceiling and took a deep breath. He turned the knob just as San popped in behind him.

"She's gone," he said from behind Adam's ear. Adam nearly came unglued.

"How does one get used to you popping in and out like that?" he asked grabbing at his heart again.

"Practice," was all he said and when Adam turned around again, he was gone.

Rattled to the core, Sarah could not speak and went straight up to the third floor and closed her door. She didn't think anyone saw her come in, but she was mistaken. Eden was still in the den and saw instantly that something was not right. She bent down to pick up a broken piece of glass that was left behind by the vacuum cleaner, and when she straightened up, San was there. Eden just stood there glaring at him with her hands on her hips.

"I don't suppose you have anything to do with Sarah's mood?"

He was trying to look at her with a straight face and broke into a grin. Pressing his lips together, he smiled and in a high-pitched voice, announced, "Guilty."

She dropped her hands from her hips with a disgusted sigh. "San! What are we going to do with you? What have you done now?" Sitting down in the chair that Adam had sat in earlier, he explained to Eden what had happened at Adam's office.

"You slammed the door in her face... without an explanation? Are you insane? What were you thinking?" she said raising her voice in frustration. She was as mad as a hornet at this point. "Well now, what do you suggest we do to smooth this over? What explanation can we possibly give her that will sound believable?" Eden was absolutely furious with him. "How can we fix this, San?"

"It's already done Little One, would you relax, please."

"Done! How is it done? I saw the look on her face just now when she got home, so you tell me... how is it done?"

"I've taken care of it Eden, I just left her, she's fine, there will be no questions, and after she has her bath, she'll come downstairs as if nothing happened."

"Are you sure, San?"

"Positive. It wouldn't be any fun being me if I couldn't fix things."

"You wouldn't have to 'fix' things if you'd behave yourself!" She was speaking through clenched teeth and using air quotes.

"You're right Little One, and I'll be more careful in the future."

"No, you won't! You're enjoying this too much!" she said, pointing her finger playfully at him.

Loving that 'mother hen' part of her, he knew she was being overly protective of Sarah. Walking over to her, it was his turn to put his arms around her. Feeling her body relax under his touch, caused him to smile, pleasingly to himself. Standing in his arms with her eyes closed, she enjoyed the feeling that his touch had always given her. Kissing the top of her head and speaking into her hair, he said, "I have to go Eden; Sarah is on her way down."

He was gone but not quite soon enough. He hadn't given her time to adjust from the comfort of his arms to facing Sarah. She was still in the soft mussy stage of the comfort of San's arms when upon opening her eyes, Sarah had walked in.

"You have the look of love on your face Mom, are you ok?" Sarah said with a questioning squint.

She was teasing Eden, but the look was there.

"Yes, Honey, I'm fine, and how was your day?"

"It was great. We learned so much in class this morning, and I had time for a long lunch before heading over to the Medical Centre. Working for Adam is giving me a great deal of experience. I would never have gotten this hands-on experience from a classroom, and he is great to work under. He is such a wonderful doctor," she swooned.

Eden saw that Sarah still had a lot of love and admiration for her husband and it showed in her expressions. Still very much in love with each other, it was worth all the sacrificing they'd done to get Adam's career launched. Sarah had sacrificed a lot for her husband, but she never regretted a moment of it.

Arriving home, Adam headed straight for the den. Hearing the door open, Sarah went to the door to greet him. Heading straight to Sarah, he gave her a hug while trying to compose himself and wondered what he'd say to fix what had happened at his office. Looking up, he saw his mother.

"Hi, Mom."

Seeing the frantic look on his face, Eden shook her head 'no' and pointing at Sarah's back and then gave him the 'thumbs up' signal while mouthing the word 'San'. Sheer relief ran through him, and it was de ja vu all over again. Memories came flooding back of standing in the Garden, the day Jacob was lost. Eden had given him the exact same signal then too. Closing his eyes, he felt relief, and when he opened them again San was standing in front of the mantle, and Adam formed the words 'thank you,' and San winked at him and was gone... Looking at his mother, he just smiled and shook his head. He envied all the years his mother had had with this character and thought how much of his shenanigans he'd missed.

~

Adam's life had taken on a whole new meaning since meeting San. He felt happy, less stressed and complete. Spending time with San was like finding a long-lost friend or relative. He'd found his father and lost him all in a matter of hours, but he had gained so much more because of it. He'd been missing so much over the years by not knowing who San really was. Yet he'd never felt alone and had always felt as though there was someone with him. That special someone was close enough so that he could even smell his scent and was always just out of his reach. He never knew exactly what the scent was until San pulled him into his arms when they'd met. It was like the music you can't quite get the words to, but the tune would not leave your brain, or he was hungry but didn't know what to eat to satisfy his hunger. There had always been longings, but since San had satisfied them, he felt like a different man.

He'd had two kinds of emotions that were as opposite as day is to night. The strain from learning about Luke being his father, then about his conception, to emphatically knowing he never wanted to see him ever again. Finding San and having him in his life, was like waking up from a foggy dream and able to finally see clearly pass the smoke.

Sarah noticed a change in her husband, but she didn't quite know how to pinpoint it. He'd changed some and in a good way. She didn't want to question it, but it was a noticeably good change. She saw that he was in a happier frame of mind, kind of light-hearted. He was more attentive with the twins by spending more time with them. He lingered at the breakfast table until they'd left for school and he was not in a big rush to get out the door and rush off to the hospital. That was the major thing she'd noticed since he'd never been home when the twins woke up. On weekends, he took his turn on call, began to share the extra hours with the new residents. Change is good, Sarah thought, at least in this case it is.

20

Changes were taking place all around them. The twins were growing like weeds and ready to begin junior high in the fall. They were pre-teens, and both were excellent students. Although they were separated most of the time in school, they shared a lot of the same classes. Each had topped their class from the day they entered kindergarten. They were not exactly bored with school, but they seemed to already know most of the subjects that were being taught, which made it easy for them to breeze through school year after year.

San spent a lot of time in the twins' room, and they did not even know he was there. Silently he watched over them and made sure their home work was done, and he spiritually encouraged them to read at every opportunity. Reading was expanding their minds with knowledge beyond their years. Eve was usually mentally prepared for San's sudden appearances. She had known him since she first opened her eyes in the hospital and smiled at him from Adam's arms. So there had never been a time when she had been without him. As a little girl, he'd rock her in the comfort of his arms and talk to her. He'd calm her in the darkness of night, read to her when she could not sleep and hold her for hours even after she's closed her eyes in sleep. There was absolutely nothing he wouldn't do for his little girl. He referred to the entire family as 'his' and that's what they would always be.

Jacob could not see San whenever he was with him, but he always felt a presence. There was never a time when he felt entirely alone, and it was a comfort to him, but it also made him curious. If someone was there, why could he not see who it was?

'People are not invisible,' he thought, *but there was an invisible person here with him, he just knew it!'* He'd felt his warmth when he sat in his brown leather chair, he smelled a familiar scent in the house, and it was everywhere not just here in his room. Then he began to wonder if it was possible to love someone you cannot see. It was a feeling like when, as a youngster, he'd see his favorite teddy bear after a long day. *'Maybe the old house is haunted!'* he thought. He didn't know whether to be excited or scared, so before he freaked himself out anymore with his own thoughts, he knew who he had to talk to...

"G-Ma?"

"Hi, Jacob, you look very serious, what's wrong?"

"Did you live here when you were a little girl, G-Ma?"

"Yes, I did Jacob, I have always lived here. I've never lived anywhere else. This was my parent's home, and when they died, they left it to me. Why do you ask?"

"Were you ever afraid of anything in all the years you've lived here?"

"Afraid? Of what, for Heaven's sake?"

Looking at his grandmother for a few seconds before he spoke, Jacob wondering if he should drop it now while he was ahead or carry on with it.

Eden asked again, "Jacob? Afraid of what?"

"Ghosts?" he answered, with a questioning look on his face. He was looking her straight in the eye when he asked her, so she knew he was serious.

"Good Heavens, child, why would you ask me that? Have you seen a ghost in this house?" Asking the question, her mind went directly to San.

"No, I haven't actually seen a ghost, but I feel one, all the time, in my room. Is my room haunted, G-Ma?"

"No, Sweetheart, your room is not haunted." Pausing for thought, she asked, "Do you believe in Angels, Jacob?"

"I believe there are Angels in Heaven G-Ma, is that what you mean?"

She thought for a moment before speaking. "Yes, there are Angels in Heaven, Jacob, but do you believe in Guardian Angels?"

"I think so. Is that what you and Eve have, G-Ma?"

"Eve and me? What do you mean by that?"

"Do you and Eve have Guardian Angels?"

"We all have a Guardian Angel, Jacob."

He was quiet and thoughtful for a few seconds. "But does your Angel talk to you?"

"That's an interesting question, what's this about anyway?"

"I hear you talking, but there is never anyone in the room with you. Eve does the same thing, and she has ever since I can remember. Who does she talk to G-Ma? Do Guardian Angels only talk to certain people? If I can feel someone in my room, then why can't I talk to them or hear them or see them G-Ma? Am I not special like Eve?"

Eden's heart nearly broke in half as she listened to her grandson ask these questions, knowing she could not answer any of them. Drawing him into her arms, she held him close and thought about every question he'd asked her. How was she ever going to give him honest answers to any of them? Pulling away slightly, he looked up at her. "I think daddy has an Angel now too, G-Ma. I've always heard you and Eve talking to somebody and now daddy talks to someone too, are there three different ones or is it the same one?" Eden was beginning to panic a little bit. How could she ever give this precious child an honest answer to the straightforward questions he was asking. There was no way around it; he just wanted answers. Just as panic was setting in, San appeared, he always knew when he was needed, and this was no exception...

Just as he appeared to Eden, Jacob straightened and stepped back from her. "G-Ma," he asked, "is my Guardian Angel here right now?"

"Why Jacob? What do you mean?"

"There's a different smell in here right now, and it just came, and it's the special smell I have in my room whenever I feel someone there."

"What does it smell like, Honey?"

"I don't really know G-Ma, it's hard to describe it, but it's kind of like what daddy smells like right after a shower. It's a fresh smell, and it makes me feel happy whenever I smell it in my room. That's when I know someone is there with me. G-Ma? Is it possible to love someone that you can't see or touch?"

Looking up at San, her eyes silently pleaded with him as if asking for his help. San knew her thoughts, but he was waiting for her to answer Jacob's last question before he made his move.

"Is it G-Ma?" His voice bringing her back to the conversation.

"Is it what, Honey?"

"Is it possible to love someone that you can't see or touch?"

Looking up at San again, he silently nodded towards Jacob, gesturing towards him indicating for her to answer the boy's question. She was speaking to Jacob but looking at San when she answered him. "Yes, Jacob, it is possible." San smiled and nodded at her and at the same time he became visible to Jacob. With a circular motion of his index finger, he gestured for her to turn him around. Without taking her eyes off San, she took Jacob by the shoulders and slowly turned him around.

"Honey, I want you to meet someone..."

"Hi, Jacob, my name is San, and I'm the one..."

"You're the one in my room!" he said with excitement in his voice.

"You smell like my room does when I feel somebody there with me!" He stopped talking suddenly and stepped away as Eden's

169

hands slipped off his shoulders. Taking a few steps forward, he was in front of San. Reaching out his hand, in a timid sort of way, he hoped if he touched him he wouldn't disappear. Slowly lifting his hand, he put it on San's hand, and his face lit up into a big smile. Jacob was relieved that he was still there, and San saw it on his face. The slightest touch on San's skin had sent a flood of feelings through Jacob. Tears of joy ran down his cheeks at finally seeing his life-long companion. Sitting on a kitchen stool, San was eye level with him. Feeling the need to hug him, Jacob walked right into his arms. As San's arms wrapped around him, Jacob felt his memory drift back to the day on the beach when he was lost. Wrapping his arms tightly around his neck, he buried his face in his shoulder. "It was you, San, you brought me home from the beach!" he said in a muffled voice. He pulled away far enough to look at him. "It was you, wasn't it?"

"Yes, it was Jacob, I brought you home, Little Man."

Reaching for a tissue, this was way too much for Eden to contain herself.

San began to speak to Jacob again. "I have to say this Jacob, and you must listen. Our meeting here today must stay between the three of us for now. This is my request, and it must be honored. Do you understand what I'm saying? Are you ok with it?" At that moment Jacob would have done absolutely anything that San asked him to do. "I'm ok with it San, you can trust me, just tell me that I'll see you again."

"You'll see me again, Jacob." Throwing his arms around his neck again, he was so happy to hear those words. Giving him a big squeeze and without realizing it, he said, "I love you, San."

San wrapped him tighter in his arms and said, "I love you too, Little Man."

Watching these two people bonding in her kitchen, Eden was overcome with emotions. *'Three down and one to go,'* she thought.

21

Sarah had graduated nursing school and had accepted a full-time position with Adam. He'd shortened his hours in ER and Out-patients so that he could focus on his practice and his home life. Usually, when Sarah's day was done, Adam got home only an hour or so after she left the office. This was a significant change for everyone in the house. At one time Adam would be gone for days on end, but that was when he was searching for something. He'd hoped to find it at the hospital by spending nearly every waking hour there. But, he never found it there and what he'd been searching for had been at home all along. Since he'd come face to face with San, his whole life had changed. He was particularly happy now than he'd ever been. Especially in his home life, because he knew that San would be there, somewhere, whether he could see him or not. He knew he'd be close by and where San was, that was where he wanted to be also. He had always been happy with Sarah and the twins, but now it was the familiar aspect that he longed for.

Sarah had stayed longer at the office than usual. She had a backlog of unfinished files that needed to be put in alphabetical order and then filed away. Adam and Rachel were already gone for the day so she could work faster with no interruptions. The place was like a tomb and deathly quiet, so she thought she would work as fast as she could and get out of there. Concentrating heavily in her work, she was unaware that someone had stepped quietly into the office. She was up and down, from her desk to the filing cabinet as she finished with each folder. She was nearly at the end of her pile when a voice broke the silence.

172

"Hello there, pretty nurse," he said. Gasping with fright, Sarah leaped to her feet in a flash. Blood rushed to her ears and pounded in her head. She wondered if her legs would to hold her up as she stared at the stranger. Reaching for the back of the chair to steady herself, she desperately tried to look calm. Her mouth had gone dry from fright, and she did not know if she could speak or not.

"Are you looking for someone in particular?" she croaked.

"Nope," was all he said.

"Then what are you doing here? The office is closed for the day."

"I know it is. I've been waiting for you."

"Waiting? Waiting for me, why?" The office is closed, and there is no one here to see you, so you must leave." She could feel panic rising up in her throat as she tried desperately not to show it. She had never seen this person around before, and she knew it was not one of Adam's patients.

"I've been waiting for you, pretty nurse."

"Me? Why are you waiting for me?" she asked again.

"I've been watching you for a long time, I see you come and go from my window. One day, when I saw you coming into the hospital, I waited at the front door for you, but you walked right by me, you didn't even say hello to me. Then I saw you get into the elevator, so I waited in the lobby to see what floor you stopped at. Then the next day I came up here and waited out there by the elevator," he said pointed behind himself, "till you got off, then I watched to see where you were going, and here you are."

Thinking she must have encountered a stalker, Sarah knew this could get really bad. She knew she had reason to panic as he continued to speak.

"I saw everyone leave this afternoon except you, so I thought you must have stayed behind to wait for me."

"Wait for you? Who are you? What do you want? You have to leave, or I'll call security," she said forcefully. She was inching her way over to the phone and noticed he was creeping closer. As she reached for the phone, his hand slammed down hard on top of hers.

"I don't think you should do that, pretty nurse." His eyes drifted to her name tag. "So, your name is Sarah, that's a pretty name."

Going into panic mode, Sarah was certain there was no way to stop it. Her heart was beating rapidly and pounding loudly in her ears until she thought she'd pass out. Feeling his sweaty palm still on the top of her hand, she didn't want to struggle and cause him to panic, too. She figured that the entire medical floor would probably be empty at this time of day, and no one would hear what was going on... but she was mistaken.

Adam was home alone sitting in the den reading and waiting for Sarah. It felt strange being home ahead of her, which was a rare occurrence for him. In his 'old life' he would still be wandering around the hospital looking for someone to fix. He was enjoying the peace and quiet and the crackle of the wood in the fireplace when suddenly San appeared. These sudden appearances did

174

not shake him up like they did at first. Now he was more or less waiting for him to appear, and in the back of his mind, he had always been waiting for him.

"Adam! You must go back to the hospital, Sarah needs you, now!" Adam jumped up out of his chair, his book falling onto the floor and he was out the door as quick as a flash. The hospital was only a ten minutes' walk, but Adam ran the distance in under five. Actually, the elevator seemed to take longer than the run.

In the meanwhile, San got there ahead of him, and as he watched what was happening, he knew that Adam was not going to make it on time, so he had to step up. Just as the intruder had grabbed the phone, he'd also grabbed Sarah by the wrist with his free hand and pulled her over to him with one quick yank.

"What is going on in here?" San roared making a quick appearance. The sound of his voice stopped the intruder in his tracks. "I asked you a question, what is going on here?" he roared again. "Let go of Sarah this instant!" Sarah had no idea who this man was, but she was never so glad to see a stranger in her life. *'He could not be with security, he was not in uniform. Then who was he?'* she thought. She guessed this was not the best time to be asking questions. She was happy that someone was there, yet she couldn't stop thinking how familiar he seemed. Looking at him with fear written all over her face, San's presence calmed her down. Sarah's hand was still pressed down on the phone while the intruder gripped her wrist. San walked over to them and put a forceful hand on the man's arm, and instantly the intruder looked like a lost puppy. Releasing his grip on Sarah, she collapsed in the chair behind her just as

Adam came running into the front office and around to where he'd heard voices.

"What's going on in here?" he panted as he looked from Sarah to San and then to the intruder. Sarah managed to get her legs working enough to get up off her chair and run to Adam. Collapsing in his arms, she cried from relief. She was so glad to see his face appear in the doorway. Confused at seeing San, Adam wasn't sure if he was visible to Sarah. Out of loyalty to him, Adam quietly held Sarah and tried to calm her fear and waited.

San spoke up and said, "I'll be right back once I get this fellow back up to the sixth floor." Sarah and Adam knew instantly that the intruder was from the psyche ward a few floors up. It was all making sense to Sarah now as she remembered him saying he had been watching her from his window. Thinking if she hadn't panicked, she might have realized that he was an escapee. She'd never encounter patients from the psyche floor. Thinking about it now, she realized she could have handled the situation differently, by remaining calm. Those people usually respond to authority figures, and once he sensed her panic, he knew he'd obtained the upper hand. Although he would not have harmed her, he'd taken advantage of her fear.

Standing beside Adam, Sarah was still shaky when San walked back in. He and Adam looked at each other for a few seconds and then Sarah broke the silence.

"Adam, how did you know I was in trouble and needed you?" Without waiting for an answer, she turned to San. "Are you with security?"

176

"No Sarah, I'm not with security," San answered honestly.

"I didn't think so, I haven't seen you around the hospital before, but then again you do seem familiar, do I know you?" San gave Adam his nod of approval, indicating that it was time to tell her. Turning Sarah around gently by the shoulders, Adam asked her to please look at him. When she looked up into his eyes, he began to speak.

"Do you remember back when I delivered the twins?"

"What does that have to do with...?" He interrupted her mid-sentence.

"This is important Sarah, do you remember?" he asked, trying to keep his voice as calm as possible.

"Yes, Adam, of course, I remember the birth of my babies!" Adam and San were sensing her frustration with all she had just gone through tonight and now facing a barrage of questions. "Do you remember Sarah?" Adam continued, "when I told you I'd always felt as though I had a Guardian Angel? And, that I was never alone?" Crinkling her forehead in question, she tried to recall, and he asked her again. "Do you remember Sarah, it's important."

"Yes Adam, I do remember, you said you had a feeling that someone was with you all the time or at least most of the time."

Relief swept over him and as he smiled at her. Taking her gently by the shoulders, he turned her back around to face San. "Meet my Angel, Sarah, this is San, San Taman. He has been with me since before I was born, and I just recently found out that he

177

knew about me before my mother did. Sarah, he has been with all of us and was with us the day the twins were born. It was San who brought Jacob home to us the day he was lost on the beach, and it was San who brought me here tonight because he knew you were in trouble."

Sarah put her hand up to her mouth to stifle a cry. With tears in her eyes and a trembling voice, she spoke to San. "You were in the room with me when I went to check on Jacob that day weren't you?"

San nodded his head. "Yes, I was Sarah, and I stayed with Jacob all night."

She took a step toward him, he opened her arms, and she walked in for his welcoming embrace. "Thank you, San, for my son's life, for Adam's life and for watching over our family." He hugged her tighter and then released her. "No thanks needed." Sarah turned back to say something to Adam and looked around, and San was gone. She looked back at Adam with a surprised look on her face.

"Don't even ask." And they both laughed.

Eden was on her way back to the den when she noticed the front door was slightly ajar. Walking over, she closed it tight and went into the den. Seeing Adam's book on the floor, she immediately sensed danger. *'This was not something Adam would do.'* Thinking something must be wrong! *'Where was he? Where did he go in such a hurry?'* Before she went off the deep end, San appeared. Sensing her agitation from the office, he left once Sarah was ok with everything that she had just gone through and what she'd learned.

Without thinking, Eden flung herself into his arms as soon as she saw him. Trying not to panic, she began telling him what she'd seen. The open door, the book on the floor, the fears she had that something was wrong.

"Slow down Little One," he said leaning against the back of the chair. "I know what happened, but there was no time to find you. Sarah was in trouble at the office, and I had to come and get Adam and then go back to Sarah. As it was, I was there ahead of Adam, but in time to stop an intruder."

"An intruder!" she shrieked. "What happened? Is Sarah alright? Is Adam with her now?" San told her everything that had happened back at the office, Sarah working late, in the office alone, and the escapee from the psyche ward, the near attack on Sarah. Eden sat in silent horror as she listened to him relate back to her what had taken place. Her only sense of relief was that she knew San was there the entire time. Although she knew that Sarah had been in great danger, knowing San was there, had eased her mind. When he finished telling her about the events of the evening she smiled at him. "Does that mean that she knows about you, too?" Smiling back at her, he nodded his head. "Then, that means that we all do!"

"Yes, it does, I'm finally and completely out of the bag... to our family anyway."

Laughing at the context he used to bring himself out, Eden was elated, knowing her family was on equal footing. Realizing there were no more secrets and her family had no reason to think of her as a complete nut any longer.

"This is the best day ever!" she said, and without a second thought, she reached up, put her hands on each side of his face and kissed him! It was not a lingering kiss, but their lips met and held for several seconds. San immediately straightened up from where he'd been leaning, and they stared into each other's eyes. The very sight of him made her heart pound even faster than it already was. San, sensing her embarrassment, knew she was feeling awkward. She'd never been more beautiful to him than she was at that moment. Lowering her eyes to the floor, she didn't know what else to do. Placing the side of his index finger under her chin, he raised her head to meet his gaze. Slowly, he lowered his head and kissed her again, while drawing her into his arms. Releasing his hold on her, they just stood there gazing into each other's eyes.

"My Goodness! What just happened here? What are we doing?" she whispered. Touching her lips with her fingertips, she turned away in a trance-like state. Before she had a chance to take a single step away from him, he touched her arm, and she stopped, turned to look at him and slowly stepped back into his waiting arms ...

Epilogue

The next day Eden began to face facts as she reminisced about being in San's arms. She'd come to realize that there couldn't be anything more between them than what they already had. She had to speak to San about her concerns.

Sensing he was needed, he appeared.

"San, we have to talk."

"Yes, Eden, I know we do?"

"Eden?" she said aloud, and almost to herself. "You haven't called me 'Eden' since I was a child. I think I prefer, Little One! But, that is not why we have to talk."

"You are making it sound more serious than it is, Eden."

"There you go again, calling me 'Eden.' This is serious, San." Pausing, she wondered how she'd say it.

"I love you, San, and I believe I always have. I looked forward to seeing you from the time you first appeared to me. From then until now, my feelings have not changed, they have only deepened. Even though I really love my family, you have been the one constant, for most of my entire life. I could not bear to live without you."

"What are you talking about? I am not going anywhere."

"I know you wouldn't want to, but you may have to."

"What makes you say that?" he said with a frown.

"We have such a special, loving relationship, and you have been unwaveringly protective of my little family. I really couldn't bear it if that had to change. We are finding ourselves in a difficult situation. Yesterday was a mistake," she said raising her hand as in defeat, "a much-enjoyed mistake, but a mistake none the less."

"I know, Little One, it is something we were going to have to talk about, and I'm glad you brought it up."

"So?"

"This has been problematic for me too, Eden. I truly don't want to jeopardize everything we have either. I truly adore your little family as if they were my very own. This is the first time, in a very long time, that I have been privileged to have my own family, and the last thing I want, is to lose it all."

"Oh, San, that is how I feel, too."

"You know I will always be here for you, and OUR little ones. As a matter of fact, I promise I will be here for your grandchildren and beyond.

"I know, and that is extremely comforting to think about. But, you will also be watching me grow old. That could be unsettling for both of us! But knowing you will be here long after I am gone is very comforting, San."

"Have you forgotten that I have been watching you grow from a little girl to a grandmother all these years. The only difference

182

that I see is that you are more beautiful, and I adore your loving heart."

"Thank you, San."

"I love you too, Little One. You will always be my special lady, even if you were more than nine hundred years old, too! So, I am happy that it will give you a sense of peace knowing I will always be here watching over your loved ones. So, stop worrying and get over here Little One, and give me a hug to seal our deal."

THE END

Other Titles by Dee

Gypsy Heart

The Grand Manor

Timeless Love

Secrets in Kanyon Ridge

Tidbits, Tips & Treasures - A Self-Help eBook

Watch for these Titles

J O Y

Then, Now & Forever

To remain in touch with Dee, contact her
through her website at
www.deelightfulreading.com

Made in the USA
Lexington, KY
10 February 2019